THE
GLADE

THE GLADE

NASEEM JAMNIA

ALADDIN
New York   Amsterdam/Antwerp   London
Toronto   Sydney/Melbourne   New Delhi

This book is a work of fiction. Any references to historical events, real people, or real places are used fictitiously. Other names, characters, places, and events are products of the author's imagination, and any resemblance to actual events or places or persons, living or dead, is entirely coincidental.

ALADDIN
An imprint of Simon & Schuster Children's Publishing Division
1230 Avenue of the Americas, New York, New York 10020
For more than 100 years, Simon & Schuster has championed authors and the stories they create. By respecting the copyright of an author's intellectual property, you enable Simon & Schuster and the author to continue publishing exceptional books for years to come. We thank you for supporting the author's copyright by purchasing an authorized edition of this book.
No amount of this book may be reproduced or stored in any format, nor may it be uploaded to any website, database, language-learning model, or other repository, retrieval, or artificial intelligence system without express permission. All rights reserved. Inquiries may be directed to Simon & Schuster, 1230 Avenue of the Americas, New York, NY 10020 or permissions@simonandschuster.com.
First Aladdin hardcover edition May 2025
Text © 2025 by Upswell Media LLC
Jacket illustration © 2025 by Marcela Bolívar
All rights reserved, including the right of reproduction in whole or in part in any form.
ALADDIN and related logo are registered trademarks of Simon & Schuster, LLC.
For information about special discounts for bulk purchases, please contact Simon & Schuster Special Sales at 1-866-506-1949 or business@simonandschuster.com.
Simon & Schuster strongly believes in freedom of expression and stands against censorship in all its forms. For more information, visit BooksBelong.com.
The Simon & Schuster Speakers Bureau can bring authors to your live event. For more information or to book an event, contact the Simon & Schuster Speakers Bureau at 1-866-248-3049 or visit our website at www.simonspeakers.com.
Jacket design by Karin Paprocki | Interior design by Mike Rosamilia
The text of this book was set in Adobe Garamond Pro.
Manufactured in the United States of America 0425 BVG
2 4 6 8 10 9 7 5 3 1
Library of Congress Cataloging-in-Publication Data
Names: Jamnia, Naseem, author.
Title: The glade / by Naseem Jamnia.
Description: First Aladdin hardcover edition. | New York : Aladdin, 2025. |
Audience term: Preteens | Summary: When twelve-year-old Pina and her friend Jo fall asleep in a haunted glade at summer camp, they enter each other's dreams and end up bringing their nightmares to the waking world.
Identifiers: LCCN 2024048871 (print) | LCCN 2024048872 (ebook) |
ISBN 9781665949804 (hardcover) | ISBN 9781665949828 (ebook)
Subjects: CYAC: Horror stories. | Nightmares—Fiction. | Camps—Fiction. | Summer—Fiction. | Iranian Americans—Fiction. | LCGFT: Horror fiction. | Paranormal fiction. | Novels.
Classification: LCC PZ7.1.J3865 Gl 2025 (print) | LCC PZ7.1.J3865 (ebook) | DDC [Fic]—dc23
LC record available at https://lccn.loc.gov/2024048871
LC ebook record available at https://lccn.loc.gov/2024048872

*Not all adults are safe for the kids in their lives.
This is for those kids. You deserve better.*

ONE

The town outside Wanderers National Park looked deserted. Screen doors swung on creaky hinges. Rusty cars with broken windows sat abandoned at street corners. Shriveled brown and gray mushrooms sprouted through a black garbage bag covered in buzzing flies.

I hugged myself, hoping there were no spiders lurking about, with their beady million eyes and hairy legs and gross webs that stuck to everything.

"Well, girls," said Mom, surveying the forest in front of us. "We're in quite a pickle."

Up the hill waited Camp Clear Skies, where my best friend and I would be away from our families for two whole weeks. Mom had objected to me attending until Baba—feeling guilty for catching me crying after he initially said no—sided with me, but that was before we'd gotten a second flat tire and couldn't find a mechanic. She regretted agreeing, I just knew it.

"It'll be fun," said my best friend, Jo, pushing up her cap to scratch her sweaty brown forehead. She was speaking to Mom but looking at me with her *I know you're panicking, but I've got you* face. We were lucky Jo's Aunt Lyd and Uncle Brock let her come with me to camp, but Jo said it wasn't luck; they were excited to have the apartment to themselves. "Don't worry, Mrs. Ahmadi. The hike can't be that bad. And I bet someone at the camp can help." Like anyone who wasn't my dad, Jo slurred our last name instead of enunciating *Ah-mahd-ee*.

Baba had given up correcting her ages ago, though, and now hoisted my suitcase. "She's right, Grace," he said to Mom, leading the way. "Kids, let's have an adventure!"

Mom's eye twitched.

Even in the daytime the dark woods looked like they'd ensnared night between their leaves. I gulped. Shadows stretched and quivered. Branches rustled and scraped. A compost-pile odor filled the air. Someone whispered my name, but when I spun around, no one was there. Mom, Baba, and Jo waited in front of me; it must have been the wind.

Before I realized it Jo had moved beside me and taken my sweaty palm. "Kaya mo ba?" she asked, using her side of our code words. I wasn't sure of the exact translation, but Jo said it was how she could make sure I was good to keep going or whether she needed to hatch an escape plan.

My response was automatic: "Khoobam." I squeezed her hand. Jo's reassurance soothed and shamed me. Camp was supposed to transform me into Pina 2.0, who wouldn't need Jo as a protector against the world. We weren't even there yet, and I was already messing up that plan.

We were rescued from a long hike when bickering voices floated toward us before a golf cart whipped into view. The driver raised a finger off the steering wheel in a wave before skidding to a stop. "Afternoon! You guys here for Camp Clear Skies?"

The driver was a dorky white teenager wearing khaki shorts, a bright orange fanny pack—a *fanny pack!*—and an orange cord around thick glasses under an orange visor. In the passenger's seat sat a scowling kid, chewing and popping gum.

"Pina Ahmadi and Jo Manalo for age group twelve," said Baba. "Our car got a flat, but we have had no luck finding a mechanic." Baba pronounced the words *ge-roop* and *fe-lat* in his accent.

"Ah jeez, that's 'cause Mr. Winters takes midday naps." The driver hopped out of the cart. "I'm Senior Counselor George. I use he/him pronouns. And this here is my little sister, Bethany, using she/her. Say, how about I take the kids up? I'll give Mr. Winters a jingle after, and take you to him and stuff."

Baba offered his hand, and George, eyes widening, reached out as far as he could to shake before quickly dropping the hand.

"Oh my God." Bethany exaggerated a sigh. She and George wore similar T-shirts, with CAMP CLEAR SKIES written above a cartoon googly-eyed campfire and s'mores. Bethany's was lime green, George's hydrangea blue. "Ms. Angela sent us for gas! We can't leave without it! If *I* was a counselor, I could drive the golf cart, but *nooo*—"

"Uff-da, you're not even thirteen," said George, except it sounded like a question. "Would one of you folks mind staying? I think I can fit the kids in the back."

"I'm almost a *teenager*," whined Bethany, who didn't

speak with the same accent as George. "I'm not a little kid—"

"That would be wonderful," interrupted Mom, sporting Mom Look #12, *Exhausted*. (To date, I'd counted fifteen Mom Looks.) "I'll join you in the front."

Baba agreed to wait for George's return, so Jo and I hopped into the back of the cart (no seat belt in sight). From where she sat, Bethany catalogued us, then sniffed. "I'm in the age twelve group too. I already know the whole camp *and* Ms. Angela—she's the owner—'cause of my dork-faced brother. I'm definitely gonna be a counselor next year. Ms. Angela said she'll make an exception for me since I already know the rules. So you'd better not break any in front of me!" She twirled her blond ponytail as she popped another gum bubble. White sunscreen streaked her nose.

Sheesh. Wasn't camp a place away from mean girls and bullies? Maybe Camp Clear Skies was no different from school. Maybe there were lots of people like Bethany. Maybe—

"Got it." Jo stood to stretch and, stepping around my feet, nudged me over so that she could sit between me and Bethany as a barrier. She called this move the *meat shield defensive maneuver*. "Pina's great with rules," Jo told Bethany, smiling as if a stranger our own age hadn't told us off for some future mistake. "We'll be on our best behavior."

But I knew that look. That was the look Jo used in front of Aunt Lyd and Uncle Brock so they wouldn't yell at her. That was the look she gave our teachers and principal whenever she got in trouble protecting me.

"Khoobee?" I asked. Our code words were perfect for moments like these.

"Mabuti." Jo gave me a thumbs-up. Bethany blew a bubble.

After settling our suitcases in the roof compartment, Mom hopped into the front beside George. "Let's see about this 'magical' camp, shall we?"

My legs jittered. Mom was referencing the camp's brochure, which promised Camp Clear Skies was a "magical" experience. If it didn't live up to her expectations, she could still take us back home, and then I'd never become Pina 2.0.

As George and Mom talked and the golf cart raced back up the hill, Jo didn't let me fret. She threw an arm around my shoulders and squeezed. She was already, like, ten inches taller than me (although I was three months older). "Pinaaaaa. Khoobee, okay? Remember how hard you worked to convince both your parents? And how exciting it was when your mom caved? Everything's gonna be great. Camp is all you've talked about for, like, three months."

"Oh my God," said Bethany. "Really?"

"Not that long," I muttered, not liking Bethany's smirk. But Jo was right. I wanted to be here, even with rude campers and unsure moms. I leaned into Jo's hug. She smelled like her strawberry shampoo.

We survived the swaying branches and inching shadows, although I grasped the edge of my seat the whole time in case a giant spider attacked. I loved nature, but none of my research into Wanderers National Park had prepared me for how . . . *off* this area felt. As we rode, I ticked through the scientific names of the trees we passed to keep calm: *Abies balsamea* (balsam fir), *Acer rubrum* (red maple), *Populus grandidentata* (American bigtooth aspen).

Sweaty handprints remained on the fake leather after I released my death grip after we pulled into a half-full parking lot. My eyes widened when I saw how many people were already here.

How many *new* people.

Had the temperature dropped? I should have taken my chances with the woods.

"Girls' cabin is over there," said Bethany, pointing. "The one near the Rec Hall. But you have to check in with Ms. Angela first! She's over there."

"I've got it." Mom waved a hand. "You two go ahead."

Getting away from Bethany? Yes, please.

I raced after Jo. Since the point of Camp Clear Skies was to explore the Great Outdoors, there weren't many buildings: two connected ones the brochure said was the Recreation Hall—housing the cafeteria and arts and crafts rooms—and two large sleeping cabins. The buildings looked pretty old, like the roofs might cave in at any second, or like they had rotting wood for walls. Could a camp be haunted?

Silly Pina, ghosts weren't real. No worrying allowed!

In front of our cabin was a long table with a bunch of markers and name tags. I alternated between purple, red, and green for my name and pronouns. Jo grabbed aqua and wrote "she/they" under her name, like we'd discussed.

"Are you sure you want me to stick to 'she'?" I asked.

She nodded. "I wanna see how it feels when other people use both. I can try it with you any—"

I waited for her to finish.

She cleared her throat. "Um. Yeah. Anyway. Let's check inside."

THE GLADE

Ooookay?

Jo opened the screen door, which slammed behind us. She peeked into the washroom off the entrance. "Oh man, I thought we'd have to go without showers! Does it smell funky in here?"

It did, but I didn't answer. *I can try it with you anytime.* That's what Jo had been about to say. So why had she cut herself off? Was Jo trying to find a nice way to tell me she wanted to make other friends and find someone she liked more than me?

I counted to ten. I was doing that thing where I got so caught up in my head that the world shut down around me, and all I could feel was my tight chest and sweaty hands and pukey stomach.

A few months ago, I read a novel about a white girl who lived in the seventh-most-haunted town in the country, and she overthought everything and constantly worried and got something called panic attacks, where her body totally shut down and all she could do was freak out. She'd used the word "anxiety" to describe when her mind raced through three hundred possibilities and focused on the worst ones. Until then, I didn't know "anxiety" was something a doctor could diagnose you with. I asked

Mom to read it so that after, I could ask her if I had "anxiety," even if I'd never had a panic attack like the character had, but she hadn't read it yet.

"C'mon, let's choose a bunk!" Jo tugged me into the middle of the room. Other than the washroom, the cabin was one large room with bunks everywhere. Bunks that were taken, because ten million cars sat in the parking lot, which meant our cabin had at least five million campers.

But there in the back—perfect. I beelined to an empty bunk next to the window, overlooking the forest. From here it looked less spooky . . . ish. At least the funny smell didn't seem as strong. "This one okay?"

"It's great!"

"Top or bottom?"

"Are you kidding? Your mom would never let you take the top."

"That's quite right," said Mom from behind us. I jumped. Gosh, she was like a cat. (I hoped we got a cat one day.) "You know I don't like you where you could get hurt, Proserpina."

Ugh. Only Mom called me by my full name. Why hadn't I gotten a normal Persian name like my big sister and dad, or a normal white name like Mom's?

THE GLADE

(At least "Persephone" was pretty, but Baba would never have let me be named after an ancient Greek goddess, not when they'd been the enemies of the ancient Persians. The Roman version of the same god was apparently okay, hence my name.)

Mom handed over a pair of bright green shirts like the one Bethany wore. She helped Jo make the top bunk as I triple-checked that there were no webs or spider sacs trapped around the mattress (ew!) before making my bed, tucking my latest read under my pillow. No haunted towns in this one; this book was about Black kids fighting the Four Horsemen of the Apocalypse.

Out of the corner of my eye, I kept watch on the forest. Books and experience had taught me nature wasn't good or evil; it just was, the way black holes and exploding stars weren't evil despite their destruction. Yet no forest I'd been in before had left me this unsettled. I couldn't pinpoint what, exactly, made me so uneasy, but instinct told me those woods—and Camp Clear Skies—hid secrets within.

TWO

Jo and I slid our suitcases under the bunk and admired our handiwork. Despite how neat everything looked, Mom pursed her lips in Mom Look #10, *How Could This Have Happened?* Impressive she'd kept it at bay this long.

"Cannot believe I agreed to this," she muttered. "A summer camp in another state! I sure hope that's not poison ivy on the walls outside."

It wasn't; it was *Parthenocissus quinquefolia* (Virginia creeper). Common mistake, but if I interrupted her, she'd lecture me about talking back.

"And it smells moldy in here. If you want to make a damping-off agent, you need to take—"

THE GLADE

"Cinnamon," I parroted. "One tablespoon for a half quart of water. Mom. I know."

She looked at me like she could consider letting me go, which was saying something. Letting go wasn't Mom's strong suit, thanks to my big sister, Pari. Could this be a new Mom Look?

Mom made both me and Jo reapply sunscreen before we headed out to see if Baba had arrived. (Jo darkened right away in the sun, but I turned pink before tanning.) Our SUV was in the parking lot, but it wasn't until we ran into Senior Counselor George that we learned where my dad had wandered. Sure enough, when we rounded the corner, Baba sat in front of the open doors of the Rec Hall with two kids, building with sticks and hot glue.

Typical Dad, making friends way easier than I could.

"Is this them? Your daughters?" said one of the kids, bouncing in their seat as Jo, Mom, and I approached. (To my relief, the wooden walls were not rotting, but the smell was back.) The name tag on the kid's camp shirt read ARISH, HE & HIM, and his pronouns were embellished with stars. Thick black hair cushioned dark sunglasses. His skin was brown like Baba's, but he looked like he was from India or Pakistan or Bangladesh. "Your dad is soooo cool!"

I made a face. My dad was a *dad*. He wasn't cool.

Jo made a face too, probably because she didn't have a dad anymore. "He's not my—"

"He said she was 'like a daughter,' you goof," said the other camper, a short Black kid wearing a shirt from the show *Unicorn Quest*. I didn't watch it, but Jo did since it came on right before her favorite show, *DynoHunters*. (Jo's cap, the one I saved up my allowance money to buy for her birthday last year, was what the main character wore.) "Your dad was teaching us about geometry and engineering," the kid continued. "I'm Eddy. My pronouns are he/him. And this guy's Arish, same pronouns."

"You know," said Baba, "your name might be the Persian name Arash. Urdu has many Persian words in it. And—"

Oh no. If I didn't stop him, Baba would go on about how the Persians had invented algebra and pants and who knew what else. (*Everything else*, Baba would say.)

Mom beat me to it. "Reza." She sported Mom Look #7, *Exasperation*. "We need to get going if we're going to reach our hotel at a reasonable hour."

The two kids trailed us as we trudged back to the parking lot. Baba shook hands with both of them, solemn looks on their three faces, and encouraged them to "keep at it." To me, he said, "Have fun, Baba-jaan," and kissed the top of my head.

Mom gave Jo and me hugs. "Be safe," she said, hands on my shoulders. "And be careful. Remember to pay attention for poison ivy, and don't scratch your bugbites or they'll get infected. And put on sunscreen every two hours. If you get hurt, your counselor can call us. You too, Jo."

"Yeah." Jo stared at the ground. "Right."

If I knew Jo, and I did, she was remembering what her aunt and uncle had said when they'd dropped her off at our place last night: *Don't bother Pina's family for anything.* Sometimes—okay, a lot of times—I wished they'd disappear. They constantly complained about Jo, even when we were in the room. If they were gone, she could live with us and never have to see them again.

My parents got in the car. "Khoobee?" I asked Jo as we waved.

She nodded instead of saying her code word back.

As the car pulled out, my shoulders relaxed. Phew!

Time to start my summer adventure. Except my stomach knotted as the car disappeared. I'd never been without my parents before. A cold wind swept through my hair.

Would I ever see them again?

Ugh. I was such a baby.

I rubbed the goose bumps on my arms and turned to the others. "Sorry about my dad. I'm Pina, by the way. I use she/her pronouns. And this is my best friend, Jo."

"She/they." Jo pointed at her name tag, back to being cheerful. "I like your hair. You get it cut recently?"

This was to Eddy, who had lightning bolts shaved into his fade. He smiled, ducking his head. "Uh, yeah, yesterday."

Eddy and Jo smiled at each other as Arish scratched his forehead. Was this flirting?

"Anyhoo, I like your dad," said Arish. "He's way cooler than mine. How long have you two been besties?"

When we were eight, Jo had found me in the park, "running away" after a bad fight with my parents. She'd talked with me and made me laugh and walked me home, and I'd dragged her inside, and that was that. I hadn't been able to stand on my own since.

That was going to change this summer.

Arish kept talking despite his question. "Eddy and I just met, but I knew he was a cool guy the moment I saw him, and I can see you two are cool girls—people," he corrected. "It's my superpower." A nod flicked his sunglasses onto his face, and he wiggled his eyebrows. "I call it my Cool-o-Meter." He shot finger guns.

If Arish could tell whether people were cool, why was he talking to me? I was so uncool, I could melt a Popsicle. I wrapped my arms around my tightening belly.

"That's a terrible name," said Eddy. I tried not to laugh at his flat expression. "You calling yourself a superhero? I thought you wanted to be a movie star."

"I *am* gonna be a movie star." Arish puffed out his chest. "But I don't want to limit my options! Like, I might do spy movies, or sci-fi movies, or—or—a space spy movie!"

Eddy snorted. Jo grinned. But while I smiled, I couldn't let go of Arish being one of the cool kids, the ones who'd be in the center of a big circle at lunch making everybody laugh. He clearly wasn't a little twerp who needed his best friend to stand up for him anytime something was hard.

A speaker fizzled and popped in the background as

a voice summoned everyone to the fire pit. Arish led the way and declared himself the leader since he was the oldest of us, turning thirteen in September, which made Jo chase him since she was the biggest. Eddy and I followed behind.

We were going to have fun these next couple weeks, darn it!

I looked around the camp to reassure myself, but my attention snagged on little details: the chipped paint on the Rec Hall's sign, the grass tall enough to tickle my calves, the wind's rasp that sounded like hushed footsteps.

The other campers gathered around the fire pit, where a bunch of teenagers wearing blue counselor shirts stood with an adult who had a megaphone. She introduced herself as Ms. Angela, she/her/hers, the owner of Camp Clear Skies. Ms. Angela, a white woman with glasses and shiny red hair in a bun, looked like my third-grade teacher.

"I am so happy to see you all," said Ms. Angela, "especially since once upon a time, I was also a camper here! I know, I know, that's when dinosaurs roamed the earth. So without further ado, for the first time in twenty years, Camp Clear Skies is open for business!"

Twenty *years*? My sister was twenty years old. Why

had the camp been shut for as long as my sister had been alive? Had something happened?

The counselors hooted and whooped, which got the rest of the group hollering. Arish put his thumb and index finger in his mouth and whistled. Gosh, he really was too cool for me; I couldn't whistle to save my life. My heart pounded against my chest. *Thud-thud-thud.*

That cold wind from earlier gusted by again. I whipped around when I heard my name—but nothing. Eddy cocked his head and mouthed, *You good?*

Oh great. He'd seen me be a scaredy-cat. I fake smiled and nodded.

Ms. Angela introduced the counselors and clapped her hands. "These next couple of weeks are about communing with nature, forming lifelong friendships, and, most importantly, having fun! Listen to your counselors and remember: this is your time to shine! We don't have a lot of daylight left"—she glanced toward the setting sun—"so the rest of the night is free time. Snacks are over here, and anyone who hasn't had dinner can find boxed sandwiches in the Rec Hall. We'll talk about what's to come over breakfast."

I clapped with the others, but nerves ate my stomach.

As the giant group splintered, Arish hollered at George that he wanted to show "non-boys" their cabin, and George, lifting his visor to scratch his forehead, shrugged and agreed.

"Where does Ms. Angela sleep?" I wondered aloud as we headed over, but the others didn't know.

Arish half ran, half skipped toward the boys' cabin to open the screen door with a dramatic bow. The boys' cabin looked exactly like the girls' cabin, except it was about a hundred times messier. The fans on the tall ceilings buzzed, scattering loose papers on one of the counselor beds. True to their name, the Virginia creeper vines that grew outside the cabin had wormed in through the log cracks, snaking up the wall. If it weren't for the obvious signs of life, the cabin could have been abandoned. It had that vibe.

"Ours looks like this too." Jo peered around. "Less smelly, though."

"It's not smelly!" protested Arish.

Jo was teasing him, but she wasn't wrong. That musty odor my mom had pointed out in our cabin lingered, but I'd also smelled it outside, so it might have been from a plant. I perked up, thinking about the specimens I'd be able to catalog.

THE GLADE

I followed Eddy to their shared bunk. Unlike Arish's top bunk, Eddy's bottom bunk was neatly made, and I sat beside him as he pulled out an action figure from under his pillow. "This is Bombshell," he said. "She's not my favorite, but my gramma said I could only bring one, and I like her colors best." Bombshell was a purple, blue, and pink unicorn with a golden horn and gold threaded through her wings.

I touched the tip of her horn. "I like how the purple is sparkly."

"Hey!" hollered Arish. "Whaddya think? Pretty good spot, right?"

Unlike my bunk with Jo, Arish and Eddy's bunk was straight smack in the middle of the room. With more people, there would be barely enough space to walk through without running into one another. But now, only half full, the high ceiling swelled as if it were home to something much bigger, something scary. Like spiders, or worse.

Sort of how the woods felt.

Despite Jo telling him it looked the same, Arish insisted on seeing our cabin. Jo offered her hand to me as we led the way. Arish told us about this sci-fi action movie he was going to make called *The Spy Who Destroyed the Galaxy*, which was about a spy who killed the Galactic Leader because the Galactic Empire was into shady stuff and was stealing from the people instead of protecting them.

"That's why at the end, the spy's gonna get a special medal from the new Galactic Senate," he said. "'Cause he was actually saving the galaxy instead of destroying it. The title tricks you, see?"

"Wow," I said, because I didn't know what else to say.

"Ta-da!" Jo opened her arms once inside. "Welcome to the girls' cabin. Exactly like yours."

Arish sniffed. "Just as smelly, too."

I giggled. If I had time, I could make Mom's cinnamon antifungal potion and make it smell like Christmas instead. (Mom grew up celebrating, so every year we drove up to see Grandma Jean and Grandpa Rick. Grandma Jean would make spice cookies, and the smell would fill the whole house.)

Now that the rest of the five million people had arrived, our cabin had become as messy as the boys'. It was also loud. I spotted Mean Girl Bethany talking with a counselor at the front.

"Our bunk's over here." Jo led us through the maze of shoes and suitcases. "By this window."

THE GLADE

"Neat view!" Arish peered out at the forest. I rubbed my arms.

Before we could settle in, a counselor yelled, "All right, campers! It's getting close to lights-out, so boys, back to your own cabins!"

"Yeah, boys stink!" shouted Bethany, which got some laughs.

"That's not nice," mumbled Eddy. "Why's it gotta be boys versus girls? Not everyone is a boy or girl either."

Jo played with the bill on her cap. I squeezed her shoulder.

"Guess we gotta go," said Arish. "See you in the morning!"

As the others left and fellow campers grabbed their toothbrushes, I steadied myself by counting to twenty. Camp had begun, and I was, somehow, already making friends. And what was most important was that Jo and I were here together, away from my parents and her guardians. Even with a few clouds, we'd have clear skies ahead.

Probably.

Definitely?

I pressed my hand against the window. Ignoring the sinking in my gut, I counted again until I felt okay. For now.

THREE

No matter how much I tossed and turned, I couldn't sleep.

I stared at the underside of Jo's bunk, replaying Mom's fears of what could go wrong at camp. Poison ivy, "irresponsible teenagers," spider bites—

Bleh. Spiders were the worst! Was it possible that spiders had snuck into my bed? To be safe, I'd brushed off my sheets before I'd climbed in, but cobwebs lined the windows. There could be a nest, a brood of eggs waiting to hatch and spill onto my face, dance over my nose, crawl into my mouth—

Gross! I rolled over. There was no way I was going to become Pina 2.0 if I was afraid of some bugs.

THE GLADE

A voice in my mind (which sounded an awful lot like Mom) said, *Technically, spiders are arachnids, not bugs.* I liked other bugs. But spiders, with their branch-like legs and way-too-fast movements, made me want to jump out of my skin. Pina 2.0 would be Pina 2-point-kaput if I got infected spider bites that landed me in the hospital and freaked out my parents and forced doctors to hook up ten thousand tubes to my dying body.

What did you expect, Proserpina? said Mom in my head. *You think you're grown up, but there's so much you don't know. The world is a big, scary place, and you're not ready to face it.*

That's right, Baba-jaan, agreed Dad, resting a hand on Mom's shoulder. *You could get hurt. Not everyone has to be a hero. You can just be Pina.*

Just Pina, useless and afraid of spiders.

My parents loomed large as they stood in their garden, my safe haven (even when Mom quizzed me on how plant roots worked and the "antifungal properties" of cinnamon). They leered at me as I grew smaller and smaller, and they grew larger and larger. Their heads and faces stretched like putty, distorting into a pixilated image. My parents opened their mouths, giant fangs dripping saliva onto their swollen lower lips. I shrank, hugging myself, as if doing so would fend off impending doom.

The itsy-bitsy spider went up the waterspout, sang a child's voice, high-pitched and sweet but also disturbing.

And then came the spiders.

They crawled out of my parents' open mouths, spilling off waggling tongues, ballooning with every movement. I fell to the ground and scrambled back as spiders the size of dinner plates touched down on the grass. My parents' jaws unhinged, peeling back to bubble spiders the way a fountain shot water. I screamed.

And launched up from my camp bed, smacking my head into the wooden slats holding up Jo's mattress.

I grabbed my pillow and buried my face into it, breathing hard as I rubbed my head. First I upset myself so much I couldn't sleep, and then I couldn't sleep without risking nightmares out of a horror movie! I didn't like horror movies for a reason!

There was no way I could fall back asleep after that. I fished out my latest library find, glad it was safe under my pillow. I couldn't possibly lose it, or Mom would flip, and so would the librarian, and I'd be banned from the library forever.

THE GLADE

An hour or more passed before I registered the light flitting across the page. Unlike my steady book light, it cast a sickly green color, pulsing like a living thing.

More horror movie stuff? Why me?

It came from the window next to my bed. I cupped the glass, squinting.

The woods were glowing, as if the plants inside were dipped in radioactive goop.

What? Trees didn't glow! Camp Clear Skies might have been far enough north to catch the aurora borealis, but the color was wrong—yellow-green slime, like from a cartoon. Maybe this was what the brochure meant by a "magical" experience.

Nah. It couldn't be *magical* magical. The woods on the golf cart ride had felt spooky, and so did the buildings, and there was that smell . . . but that was my overactive brain talking. I'd probably scared myself into seeing things.

I pressed a palm against the mattress above me. When Jo didn't respond, I pressed harder. When Jo still didn't respond, I lay down and shoved up with my feet.

Jo's head swung down, peering at me from between the ladder rungs. "Wha?" she groaned.

"Look out the window!"

Her head disappeared for a moment before reappearing. She looked more awake. "Whoa! What do you think it is?"

I wasn't imagining things! "I . . . don't know." What could make a forest glow like that? Plants couldn't naturally glow (I'd learned in one of my library finds), not unless a scientist messed with them. But was it possible to do that to a whole forest? The tree species were nothing new: aspen and birch, with lots of conifers like pine and spruce. Nothing that should glow in the dark.

Jo lowered herself from her bunk to sit on mine. "Let's check it out."

I made a noise and clapped my hands over my mouth. "We can't do that!" I whispered as loudly as I dared.

"Why not?"

"'Cause—it's—you know why!"

Jo booped my nose. "Are *the rules* worth missing out on why a whole forest is glowing, Miss Scientist? Bethany's not awake to stop us."

I chewed my lower lip since Mom wasn't here to scold me. I hated to admit it, but Jo had said the one thing that might get me to agree: a scientific mystery. Maybe I'd make

THE GLADE

a famous discovery! MAGIC PLANTS GLOW IN NATIONAL PARK, the headlines would read. DISCOVERED BY GENIUS TWELVE-YEAR-OLD IRANIAN AMERICAN!

Ha. More like NERDY TWELVE-YEAR-OLD SPOILSPORT.

But this was a chance to prove myself as someone more than a scaredy-cat that read too many books. Ms. Angela had said camp was our time to shine, and she might have meant it literally.

"I guess we can check it out real quick," I mumbled. Jo grinned.

We pulled on socks and shoes and light hoodies. Luckily, no one else in the cabin seemed to be awake. Together, we tiptoed through the hushed, dark room, peering at the counselors' beds to make sure none of them were up either. The last thing we needed was to be kicked out of camp on our first day.

I eased the screen door open and closed, since it creaked and otherwise slammed shut. Outside, the sounds of cicadas and crickets filled the air, and lightning bugs flashed yellow green against the dark sky.

The same color as the glow.

It was chilly, but the air didn't smell like dew—it

smelled a little like Baba's dirty socks or laundry forgotten in the washer that Mom had to rewash to get the smell out of. Jo grimaced, waving her hand around her nose, while I checked back over my shoulder to make sure no one was following. Stinky forests I could deal with, but getting caught would be the end.

We wouldn't go far, just enough to see where the glow was coming from. Just enough to answer my questions and rush back before anyone saw we were out of bed. Before we got in such huge trouble that Mom would never let me leave the house again, unless it was for academic after-school activities or one of the weekend classes she forced me to take.

Before we could get past the tree line, a blast of light illuminated us.

I tensed as I shielded my face. Great. We'd been caught. It was the end of my camp career before it had even begun. Mom was going to kill me.

"Hey!" Jo whisper-yelled, stepping in front of me with a protective arm outstretched. "Who's there?"

"Oh, it's you two."

The light clicked off. Arish held a flashlight in one hand and clutched Eddy's shoulder with the other.

THE GLADE

Phew! Close call. My entire body could have turned into a pile of goo with relief.

Eddy held his *Unicorn Quest* action figure and shook Arish off, scowling. "See, I told you we'd get caught! You're lucky they weren't the counselors."

Arish rubbed the back of his neck. "Did that wake you up?" He jerked his thumb toward the glow. "We came out to investigate."

"Us too," said Jo.

"Let's go," I said, "before someone else finds us." Now that someone *had* found us, I wanted to run back to safety. Eddy was right—we were lucky *they* hadn't been the counselors.

Eddy sighed. "If this ends up being a prank, you both owe me." I knew how he felt. There was no scientific explanation for what we were seeing, so it couldn't be real . . . right?

"If this ends up being a prank, I'll give you my dessert tomorrow," promised Arish. "C'mon!"

The four of us headed to the line of trees. As we drew closer, it was clear the glow was coming from farther inside, bathing the bark with its eerie shimmer. As we went deeper, the smell began to sweeten—from moist clothes to wet soil to rain, and then lighter, to floral.

The glow pulsed.

As if in a trance, I drifted toward the light. A cold breeze tickled the back of my neck. Shadows stretched around us like in the woods near town, at the base of the hill. I'd been scared then, but that was ages ago. Tonight I wanted—no, *needed*—to find the glow.

Music drifted through, the sad strumming of the Persian four-string setar my dad liked to play, and the jangles of the chains around the daf hand drum my big sister preferred. She didn't visit often, but when she did, Pari and Baba would play and sing poetry in the language I never had a chance to learn. The melody drawing me deeper into the trees tugged at those memories.

Piiiiinaaa, murmured the night breeze. *You're so close, Pina. . . .*

"Oh fer Pete's sake!" hollered someone behind us. "Hey there! Don't keep going yet!"

We froze. Any music I thought I heard cut out. My breath wheezed. The worry I hadn't felt as we searched rushed back, like a wildfire burning debris to allow for new growth. Except what grew inside me was panic.

This was it! We were going to get kicked out. Mom

THE GLADE

would never let me go to any other camp ever again (Mom Look #9, *Disappointment*, or #15, *I Expected Better from You*). Baba would say his usual *Your mother's right, Babajaan, and this is why she makes the rules* and shake his head and say I'd broken his trust. I'd be locked at home forever.

Twigs snapped before we heard a crash, and Senior Counselor George stumbled into view.

I reached for Jo's hand, though mine was sweaty. An invisible band around my shoulders tightened. *Trou-ble*, my heart seemed to beat. *Trou-ble*.

George halted and brushed himself down. Despite being late, he wore his signature fanny pack, a cap with a headlamp over it, and a vest with many pockets. In what seemed to be usual George fashion, everything was orange. "What the heck are you four doing here? It's not safe to go out at night, dontcha know!" He wagged a finger. "You should be in bed, getting a real good night's sleep!"

Sheesh. Why did George have to be such a capital *G* Good Guy?

"But, George," said Arish, "how could we see this and not check it out?" He gestured at the glow. "I mean, aren't you curious?"

George paled, though it could have been a trick of

the many lights. "Oh yah . . . sure . . . yah, no. It's fine." His voice sounded higher than normal. The Adam's apple in his throat bobbed before he shot Eddy a Disappointed Teacher Look (not quite as harsh as Mom Look #9). "Gosh darn it, I expected this kind of behavior from Arish, but not you, Eddy. You gotta keep him in line."

Eddy flinched. I frowned. It didn't feel fair to put that responsibility on Eddy. They'd only met earlier today (yesterday?)—why did Eddy have to be in charge of Arish?

Arish rubbed the front and side of his neck. "Aww, George, it's not his fault—"

"And you two," George said to me and Jo, "should really know better, being girls 'n' all."

That felt extra unfair, especially because Jo might not have been a girl—but even if she was! Jo hugged herself, shoulders hunched, a shape I knew well from when Aunt Lyd and Uncle Brock were around.

Jeez. We might have been breaking rules, but George's freak-out felt excessive.

(A funny thought, coming from me.)

I put an arm around Jo's shoulders, but before I could check in with our code words, George added, "Now, I'm real sorry to have yelled at you guys like that, but Ms.

Angela could have caught you. Her cabin is in these here woods. But heck, I guess if you head back to bed right now, I won't tell her, and we can forget this happened."

George looked expectant, and when none of us said anything, he nodded and led us away without more scolding. The walk back somehow felt longer than going in, and by the time the trees thinned out, Jo and Eddy were yawning, Arish was rubbing his eyes, and I was ready for bed.

I glanced over my shoulder for a final look. The glow wavered, dimmed, and surged, as if it noticed me too.

As if it were staring back.

FOUR

During breakfast, while my head drooped into my plastic cereal bowl and Jo yawned beside me, Arish slid into the seat across from us. "Good morning, rays of sunshine!" His secret agent glasses were on top of his head. "How did we sleep?"

"He's been like this all morning," grumbled Eddy, sitting beside Arish with less fanfare, poking at his eggs and bacon. He didn't seem hungry. I understood how he felt. Mom never bought sugary cereal at home, and here I was letting my Cookielicious Crunch get soggy. It didn't help that the old socks smell was back, although the stink of bacon grease mostly masked it.

THE GLADE

"I don't know about you," said Jo, "but I couldn't sleep great after." She lowered her voice. "What do you think was out there?"

"Maybe the plants are fancy." Arish wiggled his fingers.

I yawned, which made the others yawn too, and shook my head. I'd already thought over the possibility before I fell back to sleep. (No more nightmares, thankfully.) "Plants aren't naturally bioluminescent."

Arish cocked his head. "Bio—what?"

I spun my spoon in my cereal. "Bioluminescent. It means a living thing that gives off light." I clenched and splayed my free hand like blinkers. "You know how some jellyfish look glow-in-the-dark?"

"Ooh, we saw those at the Shedd!" Jo clapped her hands. "That's the aquarium in Chicago. The one in Milwaukee, where we're from, is kind of small."

Our day trip to Chicago with my parents last month had been super fun, although Mom had complained about traffic the whole time and Dad made a lot of terrible fish and sea puns.

"Jellyfish and some other marine creatures naturally glow," I said. "But for a plant to glow like that, a scientist would have to change it in a laboratory. So whatever's going on isn't natural."

Arish yawned, which set off another yawn parade. "Before George found us, I thought I heard—okay, this sounds silly now, but . . ." He fidgeted. "So there's a song from this Bollywood movie with Aamir Khan that my biggest sister likes, even though my other sisters say Pakistani dramas are way better, and—"

"Sorry, did someone say my name?" Good Guy George swung a long leg over the bench, squatting near but not close to me. I startled. Where had he come from? "Did you four sleep okay?" George gave us a knowing look.

"Barely," said Jo.

"Did you?" I asked.

"Can't complain," said George.

Jo crunched her last piece of bacon. "Why were you out last night, anyway?"

George laughed, but it sounded forced. "Welp!" He slapped his knee. "I s'pose I'd better get going—"

"Ooh, ooh!" Arish pushed up. "South Asians are great at Minnesota goodbyes! C'mon, George, let's hang out by the door for four hours, and you can tell me all about last night."

THE GLADE

"Uff-da, leave it go!"

"Don't tell me you're trying to turn them into geeks like you," interrupted Mean Girl Bethany, sneering as she stood behind George. I knew that look—Megan O'Halloran and her minions gave me that look when Jo wasn't around.

George swung his leg back over the bench so that he was sitting properly but facing the other way. "Beth—"

"Nope!" She held up a hand. "I don't wanna know. Ms. Angela asked me to come get you for a counselor meeting." She preened. "Ms. Angela can rely on me, unlike *some* people."

"Yah, no, for sure." George smiled at his little sister—I guess he liked her, even though she was a jerk—and stumbled up, knocking against the bench and me. "Ope, lemme just sneak right past ya here. Okey dokey, then!"

"Well, that was suspicious," said Arish, popping his shades over his eyes as they left. "How come George talks like a Minnesotan and Bethany doesn't?"

"Aren't you the one from here?" asked Eddy.

"I'm from the Cities," said Arish, before adding, in an accent like George's, "Dese guys are from up nort'. Don't ya know dat, den?"

His ridiculous impression helped distract me for three seconds from the *I didn't get enough sleep* nausea, though it could have been *the trees are calling me* nausea.

"I wonder if he would have told us anything," I said. Maybe George knew more than he claimed.

"He probably would have," said Arish cheerfully. "Minnesotans don't get angry the way he did last night, or at least don't show it like that. If we'd badgered him, I bet he'd have felt guilty enough about the yelling to open right up. Whatever he knows must be bad."

Well, that wasn't comforting.

"We can try to get it from him later." Jo sipped her orange juice. "C'mon, you gotta eat. We're gonna have so much fun today, you'll see." She elbowed me and smiled.

I tried to smile back. Jo was right. We could find out the mystery of the glow another time.

Even if there was something more going on.

Our day started with an icebreaker. When it was her turn, Bethany shared her fun fact: her dad said the 1969 moon landing was faked, which meant there was no real evidence of the Earth being round. Ms. Lee, my fourth-grade teacher, had shown us a video of Neil Armstrong

THE GLADE

taking a small step for man, and Bethany's ideas didn't match up with that. I also weren't sure how it was a fun fact about *her*—until she added that she was sure aliens were real.

The others found it funny, but I felt weird laughing with them. They kept turning their noses up at me and Jo. When Jo's turn came around, a handful of girls whispered and stared at her ripped jeans. They were her only pair, and they'd ripped when she'd gotten into a fistfight with Joseph Collins after he'd shoved me into a locker. Her aunt and uncle hadn't replaced them, because jeans were too expensive, and yelled at her for ruining them in the first place.

Some of the other campers seemed nice, though. While we hiked that morning, we talked to a few: a Korean girl named Constance and a white girl named Mackenzie, who both used she/her pronouns, and a Black kid named Kiki with colorful beads in their braids who used they/them pronouns. The woods were way less spooky in the daytime with a bunch of loud kids, and the air smelled fresh and clean. At lunch Kiki made Jo laugh so hard, she spit up her water, and that might have made me jealous if I wasn't busy laughing too. Constance asked to sit together during parachute games, and we spent afternoon arts and crafts together too.

Afterward it was quiet time, which meant an hour and a half to ourselves. Jo passed out, but I stayed up talking with Mackenzie. She had two older brothers and lived with her dad; he'd recently introduced his boyfriend, who Mackenzie really liked. Her bunkmate interrupted us and dragged her away, but it was nice while it lasted.

I hugged myself after she left. Why was it so difficult to talk to kids at school when I could talk to other campers? Was it because my classmates had known me forever and knew I was a loser? People like Joseph Collins and Megan O'Halloran called me a nerd because I spent recess in the school library with Jo, but we were trying to get away from people like *them*. Besides, was it so bad to be a nerd if it meant I could read books with my best friend? Why was being a nerd a bad thing?

So I did what nerds did and returned to the book under my pillow, which was unfortunately beginning to smell like the rest of the cabin. Before long Bethany strutted inside like she was the queen of camp and loudly proclaimed that Ms. Angela wanted everyone at the campfire.

THE GLADE

As Jo struggled awake, I changed into my camp T-shirt. It was time for the Big Weenie Roast.

"What's a weenie roast?" asked Arish, plopping next to me on the thick grass near the campfire. It was the first time I'd seen him since breakfast. Jo had gone looking for soda. "Sounds pretty American."

"I think it is." When I stretched, the friendship bracelet I'd made earlier (with a matching one for Jo) slid down my forearm. Kiki and Constance had showed us how to braid the colorful strings, and I definitely wanted to make more. "Where is your family from?"

"Pakistan." He cocked his head. "What about you? Your dad is Persian?" He must have remembered my dad's annoying comment yesterday.

I touched my thick, wavy brown hair that frizzed when I brushed it and dug my nails into my palms to stop myself from smoothing my bushy eyebrows. Okay, it was a unibrow, but I hated that word since the bullies used it. Baba said one eyebrow was beautiful in Persian culture, but was that true when I also had his big Persian nose? I hadn't noticed these things until Jessica Connolly, one of Megan's minions, pointed it out and everyone laughed. Grandma Jean called me and my sister her "exotic little grandbabies," so maybe she'd noticed. I didn't *feel* "exotic"—I felt like me. That word made me think of souvenirs my dad brought from international business trips.

"Yeah, from Iran." I watched the clouds drift across the darkening sky, the sun beginning to set.

Growing up, before he came to the US for high school, Baba would go stargazing with his cousins. Sometimes I wondered what it was like to grow up in Iran, where other people might look like me. But then they wouldn't be American, so I'd still be different.

"He met Mom in college when she decided to become Muslim," I added. "Hey, do you speak Urdu? I don't speak Farsi, but I can understand some of it. We have the same alphabet, I think." It was specifically because I didn't speak Persian that my code word with Jo was "khoobam," "I'm good." It was one of the few phrases I did know.

"Yup." Arish patted my arm. "My aunts make fun of my accent," he admitted. "They say I sound American. My mom's side is Punjabi, and they speak way too fast for me to understand. I bet your dad's family makes you feel bad for not speaking Farsi. We're too Pakistani or Iranian for the Americans and too American for the Pakistanis and Iranians."

No one had acknowledged anything like that to me before. Jo was different; her dad died overseas when she was a baby, so no one expected her to speak Tagalog. She was raised by her white mom's family in Wisconsin, without contact from her dad's in the Philippines.

(Jo didn't believe her dad's family hadn't tried to contact them. Aunt Lyd swore that none of "those people" had ever reached out, how they'd "abandoned the mutt" in the family. I didn't get it—Jo wasn't a dog—but regardless, Aunt Lyd's words sucked.)

I didn't speak to my relatives in Iran very often, so it didn't matter that they teased me for not speaking their language. Right? At least, it didn't feel fair to talk to Jo about that, not when she went home and heard how she was "no good" and had "ruined their lives."

"Yeah," I said, lying on the grass.

If I closed my eyes, I could focus on the smell of dirt and growing things instead of the damp clothes stink that was everywhere. I could focus on the music that rose from the earth in a gentle hum, the same melody I heard last night.

My eyes flew open. The music stopped.

I must have imagined it. I should have taken a nap like Jo had.

The megaphone crackled. I raised my chin to see Ms. Angela standing in the middle of the loose circle of campers. "Hello, everyone! How was your first full day at Camp Clear Skies?"

People around us cheered. Arish cupped his hands around his mouth and let out a whoop.

Ms. Angela beamed as the noise died down. "Excellent! Tonight we have one of my favorite traditions, our Big Weenie Roast!" She gestured to the table that the counselors were setting up with condiments, buns, and bundles of hot dogs before giving us instructions. She pointed to George, who was building a fire in the pit. "If you're not comfortable roasting your own hot dog, George can help. We have more than enough for everyone, so dig in!"

Arish jumped up and offered me a hand, but I shook my head. The grass was nice. "I can wait until the line dies down. I ate a million snacks today." Mom would have lectured me on my food choices, but Mom wasn't here.

After Arish left, Jo plopped down beside me. "Hey."

"Hi." I pushed up onto my elbows. "Where were you? I thought you were gonna get a drink."

"I was, but Bethany is policing everyone and said it wasn't time yet, and then I ran into Eddy, and we talked about *Unicorn Quest*. You know it's from the same studio that makes *DynoHunters*? No wonder I like it so much!"

My lips twitched until I couldn't hide my grin. "Yeah?"

Jo looked away, her ears turning pink. Jo didn't get embarrassed very often, and her skin was dark enough to hide a blush. Her ears were the giveaway. "What?"

"What, what?" I sat up. "Do you *like* like him?" For as long as I'd known Jo, she'd never liked anyone like that: not a boy, not a girl, not the two nonbinary kids in our class. Jo'd never talked much about it, but since it was hard to make friends, it felt kind of nice that Jo might like someone.

It also made me a little jealous to share her, but I pushed that thought away.

Jo buried her face in her arms. "Well, what about you? You and Arish looked comfy."

I looked in the direction Arish had gone, but he'd disappeared into the crowd. I shrugged. "He's nice, and his family are also immigrants." I'd also never *like* liked anyone before. Boys were whatever, girls were whatever, nonbinary kids were whatever—the only person I'd ever gotten close to was right next to me. I didn't even get celebrity crushes like my classmates. All I wanted was to read my books and study plants and hang out with Jo.

"Okay." Jo picked at the grass. "You'd tell me if that changed, right?"

"Of course I would."

"Cool." She hesitated. "Uh, Pina . . ."

Her stomach growled.

She pressed a hand to it. "Never mind. I guess I'll go wait in line. Coming?"

The line looked—impossibly—longer. Then my own stomach gurgled. So much for those snacks. "Yeah, okay." Then, to be sure: "Khoobee?"

A thumbs-up. "Mabuti!"

Constance was the last person in line before we joined, so we talked to her about cheesy Korean-style corn dogs, which sounded delicious. It took a lot longer than it should have to get a hot dog, roast it, put on condiments, get chips, get soda, and look for a place to eat. Arish shot up a hand and waved frantically at us, so we went to join

THE GLADE

him and Eddy since we'd lost Constance anyway. Eddy told us Arish was on his third dog already.

"Who knows campfire songs?" asked one of the counselors.

"That's boring," said Bethany, as if anyone cared what the campers thought. "We should tell ghost stories!"

"There's no such thing as ghosts," said George, roasting another dog. We were close enough to the fire to see the char marks but far enough to not feel the heat. "Probably too big a group to play Duck, Duck, Gray Duck. Campfire songs it is! Let's see, how 'bout we sing 'Down by the Bay'?"

Bethany huffed and crossed her arms, but the counselors began to clap as George led us through the mysteries of the bay. I focused on eating, but Arish put down his plate to join in.

Down by the bay . . . where the watermelons grow . . . back to my home . . . I dare not go!

It made me think of hearing "The Itsy-Bitsy Spider" in my dream last night. I shuddered.

"Ugh, this is for babies," said Bethany, trooping over to sit with the girls who had laughed at Jo earlier. "You guys hear the story of why the camp originally closed? It's, like, a local legend. I grew up around here, so I know *all* the camp's secrets." She sounded super smug.

If Bethany knew the camp's secrets, did that also mean she knew about the glow? I nudged Jo. "What?" she said.

I nodded toward Bethany. "Listen." Although I didn't like horror movies, ghost stories were silly enough to not be *too* scary. Most of the time.

Have you ever seen a llama . . . wearing a pajama . . . down by the bay?

"Okay, listen up." Bethany straightened, probably enjoying the attention. "Super long ago, in a universe far, far away . . ."

"We're on Earth, hel-*lo*," said another Mean Girl Camper. "You're such a dork."

Bethany scoffed. "Whatever. *Wars in the Stars* is *so* mainstream. You should hear my geek brother rant about it." She wrinkled her nose in George's direction.

There seemed to be a pattern with bullies and thinking nerd things were uncool. It must have been a boring life for them. Why couldn't someone like both nerdy and popular things? "Anyhoo, as I was saying . . ."

Arish and Eddy noticed we weren't eating, and Arish stopped singing long enough to listen in.

THE GLADE

"So this took place forever ago. Twenty or thirty years or something." Bethany noticed there were more people outside her group paying attention, so she raised her voice with a smirk. "Apparently, this place"—she swept her arm to gesture at the landscape—"was a paradise back then. Full forest, grass up to your waist, clean air with no pollution, an' stuff. The point is: kids were lining out the door to come here every summer. The camp had way more interest than room for years and years. This was not a place about to shut down. Then . . . the final summer happened."

Enough people had stopped singing for the counselors to end the song and tune in. "Hey there, what's happening in the orchestra pit?" called George, who had stood to lead the clapping and singing. (I'd half expected him to bust out an acoustic guitar.)

"We decided to share scary stories," said Bethany. "You know, about the kid who went missing?"

Gosh, that was different from a ghost story. Now everyone was listening. "Someone went missing?" asked one of the younger campers, sounding nervous.

George tugged on his collar. "Ah jeez, we don't really talk about—"

"Don't be such a wet blanket." Bethany flipped her ponytail over her shoulder in her signature move. "Everyone says the woods here are weird. Remember Mrs. Gordon's son? He said there's a fairy ring that takes you to a magic world." She snorted. "As if! Probably someone living off the grid like Daddy wants to do. You're ruining my story!"

A magical world? That glow last night had sure seemed magical. But the idea was so ridiculous, I wanted to roll my eyes. There had to be a rational explanation.

George looked even paler than usual. "I don't think—"

"Oh fer cryin' out loud!" snapped Bethany, sounding so much like George it startled me. She composed herself and changed back to how she usually talked. "Can't you chill for once? It's a *story*. We're trying to have fun! Something you clearly don't know anything about."

Her minions giggled.

I tapped my fingers against my thigh. Ghost stories were okay because there was no solid scientific evidence to suggest ghosts were real, but real kids *did* go missing.

Thank goodness Mom hadn't learned about this before signing me up.

THE GLADE

"C'mon, George, we wanna hear!" said one of the older campers. "Sca-ry! Sto-ries! Sca-ry! Sto-ries!"

Some of the others on the boys' side picked up the chant. "Sca-ry! Sto-ries! Sca-ry! Sto-ries!"

Soon, half the group was chanting, and George threw up his hands and turned to the other counselors. "Fer cripes' sake! Aren't any of you gonna stop this?"

"Aw, lighten up, George," said one of them. "Could be worse. It's just some good fun."

"Yeah, c'mon, George," said another. "It won't hurt the rebranding effort. Let her finish."

George didn't look happy but sat back on the grass. Did he dislike scary stories too, or was there another reason he didn't want us to hear?

I sort of wish he'd put up more of a fight. Turning a real-life tragedy into a scary story felt disrespectful. Also, George's hesitation worried me, like he knew something the rest of us didn't.

"*Any*hoo . . ." Bethany summarized the story up until that point. "That final year the camp was open, people said something changed. The woods started to call to them, and those who went in came out . . . different."

No. There was no way. No way the woods had said

my name last night. Nighttime voices were funny, not supernatural.

"Call to them how?" asked someone in the crowd.

"What d'you mean . . . different?" asked someone else at the same time.

"Whispers in the night?" suggested one person.

"Maybe they were possessed."

"Visions no one else could see?" suggested another.

"What, like, by a demon? No way, demons don't exist."

"All that and more." Bethany's eyes gleamed. "Some said their dreams were full of monsters. Others felt hands grabbing them when no one else was around, trying to drag them into the forest. Some saw things no one else could, with promises of more if they followed the visions. When people hiked, they'd hear music. Every day that summer, kids complained about not being able to sleep well . . . because they kept waking up to bangs and scratches. Those who investigated stopped acting like themselves and wouldn't talk about what they saw, as if it was too horrible to describe."

How much of this was Bethany making up? If the locals talked about it, there had to be some sort of truth to the story, right? Plus, the woods *did* glow.

THE GLADE

Arish paled in the flickering light of the campfire. "Music?" he whispered.

I'd heard music too . . . but I overthought everything.

My stomach flipped, the hot dog and chips tossing around. If only George had put a stop to this!

"And then, at last, came the final camper. A lot of mystery surrounds who they were. Some say they weren't a camper, but a warning: the ghost of a kid who'd gotten lost long ago. Others say they were a sacrifice to keep the hungry trees away. And there are those who say the kid was the reason the forest called to others, because they were lonely and wanted a friend to play with. One thing's for sure: a kid walked into the woods and never came back out."

The gentle breeze turned needy, plucking at our hair and clothes, making the fire dance. It sung in my ear like a dream.

The itsy . . . bitsy . . . spider . . .

"They ever find the body?" someone asked.

George jumped up. "Holy buckets! Who said anything about a body?"

"A kid went missing," said someone else. "So if that's true, something had to have happened."

"Aliens," said Bethany. Her face was totally serious. "That's what I think. How else could someone go missing without a trace?"

Great, this again. From everything I'd read, it *was* likely that alien life lived somewhere in the universe. (One of my library books explained that bacteria was everywhere—on our skin, in our guts, even in the soil. Scientists had found about forty thousand species, but they thought there might be millions or billions more. That meant the likelihood of bacteria being on other planets was high.) But Bethany definitely meant the flying saucer type of aliens, and those probably didn't exist.

"Aliens aren't real," said one of the campers.

"My daddy says that's what the government wants you to think," countered Bethany.

Oh, brother. Baba said that people in the US who distrusted the government hadn't lived in countries where the government controlled every aspect of life. Mom had said a "healthy degree of skepticism keeps ruling bodies in check," whatever that meant.

"*Anyway!*" snapped Bethany, probably because she wasn't the center of attention anymore. "The real mystery is, who was the kid? Where did they come from?

And if they did walk into the woods and never came out, why hasn't anyone found anything? That's why I think it's alien—"

"That's enough."

Ms. Angela stepped into the firelight. When had it gotten so dark? Flames glinted in the reflection of her glasses, and her nostrils flared. Her expression lay somewhere between Mom Look #11, *Stern*, and Mom Look #8, *Anger*. I wrapped my arms around myself and squeezed.

But Ms. Angela sounded fine when she continued. "We're not trying to give people nightmares over here! It's time for lights-out, anyway. Please throw away your trash in the bins before heading back to the cabins. We have a busy day ahead of us tomorrow!" Then she called to Bethany and did that thing grown-ups did where they tried to hide being upset by pressing their lips together in a smile that wasn't a smile. I watched as Bethany skipped over, oblivious to Ms. Angela's mood. Or maybe I read it wrong.

Groans filled the air as people shuffled to leave. I waited so it wouldn't be crowded by the trash cans, watching as Ms. Angela led Bethany out of sight. I also waited because Bethany's story was running through my head, and I needed to catch my breath like I'd actually been running. Kids went missing in big cities like Milwaukee and Chicago, but kids going missing from small towns, where everyone knew everyone else, felt scarier.

How much of that story was true? How many secrets were in the woods?

FIVE

The next morning I'd barely gotten my bowl of cereal before Arish jumped next to me in the breakfast line, nearly knocking me over. "Listen," he said without apologizing. "Me and Eddy have been talking, and we gotta check out the glow again."

"Good morning to you, too," I grumbled. I hadn't slept well, my dreams haunted by ghost kids with no mouths and black holes for eyes, singing campfire songs. Plus the root cellar smell of the camp made me queasy (until my body got used to it by midmorning). And, to make matters worse, Jo had gone on to breakfast without me and was sitting with Eddy already. What was I, chopped liver? Yuck! "Can't this wait?"

"Nope." He beamed as if I weren't a grumpy Gus. "'Sides, you're the slowpoke today. The rest of us already got our food. C'mon!"

Accepting my fate, I followed him to the others. Jo patted the seat beside her, which made my shoulders relax.

"Morning," said Eddy, holding his action figure. "Do you watch *Unicorn Quest*, Pina? We were talking about the episode where Glitterhorn got their wings."

"Forget about that," said Arish. "We gotta talk about the plan for tonight before we split for the day."

"What plan?" Jo munched a piece of bacon. We ate turkey bacon at home, so regular bacon stank (even if it was the only thing stronger than the camp smell). Mom said the smell made her think of Grandma Jean and Grandpa Rick, who insisted on bacon for breakfast whenever we visited and got mad when Mom said no. Mom liked to say she and Dad might be Ramadan Muslims, but at least she avoided pork.

"Eddy and I were talking, and we gotta go back to that place in the woods. With the glow and music?"

"I didn't hear any music, but I thought I smelled

my mom's perfume." Eddy picked up his action figure, flapping Bombshell's wings. "I'm having weird dreams. Haven't been able to sleep much. When I wake up, I keep thinking I'm seeing that glow again."

"You've been passed out every night." Arish mimed sleeping while fake snoring loudly.

Eddy smacked his arm. "Shut up, I don't snore."

Arish peeked open an eye. "You sure?"

"Ha, ha." Eddy folded Bombshell's wings back. "The dreams are weird, like I said. They aren't nightmares," he added hastily. "I'm not a *baby*. But I feel like I'm gonna keep having them unless we check it out."

Nightmares weren't for babies, but I didn't want to think about mine. First the spider dream, then dead kids. Speaking of... "You're not worried about the missing kid?"

Eddy shrugged. "That was ages ago. They probably ran away from home or something. It's not like there's anything supernatural in there. I just want to see what it is so I can sleep better."

"That makes sense," Jo cut in before I could respond. "I thought I saw the glow last night too. What do you think, P?"

I chewed on my lower lip, no Mom here to stop me

even if it bled. This was my summer of adventure, and though it scared me, I *was* curious. The glow couldn't be natural, so was it a prank the counselors had cooked up? Why hadn't any of the other kids mentioned it? Was there something special about us?

Yeah, right.

"What about Ms. Angela?" I asked.

"What about her?" asked Arish.

"Her cabin is in the woods," said Eddy. "Not sure where."

"Then we gotta scope it out," declared Arish. I wish I felt as confident. "We can ask around today, make sure we avoid it."

Jo turned to me, expectant, and I chewed my lip again. "Okay. Why don't I be the lookout?"

"Are you sure?" asked Jo.

I nodded. "I can keep an eye out for"—I looked around since he tended to pop up when we didn't want him to—"George, and give everyone time to escape if we need to. Being careful means I'm a natural lookout."

And, I didn't tell her, I could prove to my overactive brain that my worries were silly and that I could have fun despite them. The back of my neck tickled. Something told me the glow wanted me to find it. That was freaky, but maybe the feeling would go away once I discovered its source.

After lights-out the four of us crept out of our beds and met up near the tree line. "Everyone remember to stuff your bunks?" asked Arish. "Hiding your tracks is rule number one of being a spy."

Eddy scoffed. "I don't think it's gonna trick anyone."

"I don't know about the rest of you," said Jo, "but I don't wanna put this off any longer." She held back a branch so I could step under it.

"Me too," admitted Eddy. He'd looked so determined at breakfast to stop his nightmares. I shivered despite my hoodie.

No one asked what *I* thought as we headed deeper. They probably already knew I was scared. I didn't want to dream more spider fountains or missing kids. And what would my plan be if George *did* catch us? Or, for that matter, Ms. Angela? (We'd learned her cabin was in the woods, away from the main camp, but so what?)

When I caught Jo's excited expression as she stomped me a path, I swallowed my complaints. I didn't want to be a party pooper.

There had to be a scientific explanation, and figuring it out would help.

Even if we were probably breaking a million rules.

And that Mom would have me locked up forever if she learned what I was doing.

It had gotten dark real quick. My breaths wheezed. My numb fingers trembled, although it wasn't that cold. I hoped the glow would start soon so we could hurry back. At least the smell softened the deeper we went.

"Rot," I said.

Jo turned to me. "Huh?"

"The smell around the cabins. I was trying to think of what it was. Here"—I gestured around us—"it smells more earthy. But in the buildings it's like—you remember when my dad found that mold in the community center?"

Jo wrinkled her nose. "Oh yeah. It stank something funky for months." Then she grinned wickedly. "Maybe it's the kid that went missing. They never found the body, remember?"

Arish whipped around. "You mean we might find a nasty, rotting corpse?"

"To be fair, the corpse has probably decomposed by

now," I pointed out. "If it existed." Relying on science felt better than pondering what had actually happened to the missing kid.

"Besides, I thought you were gonna be a big movie star," teased Eddy, shoving Arish a couple steps. "Can't handle a little action?"

"This is different!" After a moment, Arish grinned. "You gonna be my sidekick?"

"Maybe." Eddy paused for effect. "That is, if you're not a big baby about going into the woods at night."

"I'm not afraid of going into the woods!"

"Oh yeah?"

"Keep your voices down," I whisper-snapped, looking over my shoulder in case George should appear.

"Pina's right," said Jo, which made my chest grow warm. "Wait—do you hear that?"

We stopped walking and listened. At first I only heard crickets and croaking frogs and an owl's hoot. But then—

"Music," said Arish.

"I hear a . . . party?" Eddy sounded uncertain.

"This is what I heard the other night." My heart hammered in my throat, as if it could break through my ribs and splat on the ground.

The melancholy melody plucked from my memories drifted around us.

A flash of confusion or hurt (or both?) flitted across Jo's face. I reached to squeeze her hand. "Khoobee?"

"I hear a lullaby," she said. "What's going on?"

"Follow the musical road," said Arish. "I think it's coming from this direction."

The sounds—jumbled voices and garbled laughter, music that was different to each of us—grew louder as we walked. After a million years, Jo parted a curtain of leaves, and the sounds cut out.

In the middle of the forest sat an empty meadow, its short grass ringed with flowers. No stumps or logs, no leafy bushes where animals could hide, as if someone had cleared it out, but no signs of who or why. The grass was a pale green, not rich and dark like it should have been in full summer. Maybe it wasn't grass. It looked like moss. The air felt different too, almost misty, and smelled like heavy perfume. I yawned, a little dizzy. I wanted to bury my face into the fuzzy ground, curl up, and dig my fingers into the dirt—

"Pina?" Jo nudged me with her foot. My face was inches away from the ground, and it was definitely grass, not moss. When had I squatted? My head hurt.

THE GLADE

Jo helped me back up, but I got sidetracked again, this time by the flowers at the edge of the clearing. They were not flowers. They were mushrooms.

I knelt to examine a green-yellow one, careful not to touch it in case it was poisonous. I did recognize *Gomphus floccosus* (scaly vase chanterelles), which caused belly aches so were best avoided, and the orange caps of *Hypomyces lactifluorum* (lobster mushrooms), which could be eaten when freshly foraged; the inky caps of most *Coprinus* species were also edible—and not in season, yet somehow were growing alongside the others! And none of them were the types of mushrooms that fruited in rings, but that's undeniably what this was: a ring of different fungal species circling the clearing.

The earthy perfume was sharper down here, like rain and wet soil and the smell of fruit on the edge of being overripe. My temples pulsed, then calmed, and I yawned again. I was obviously too tired to be up; I could have sworn a mushroom twitched, puffing lavender powder around us. . . .

"Ey, P, stop investigating and hang out with us!" Jo waved over from the center of the clearing, where she, Arish, and Eddy had made themselves comfortable.

Had none of them noticed how strange this place felt? Not a bad strange, but still, strange. Like I'd taken a lot of cough syrup and was on the edge of falling asleep. What was I concerned about again?

I pinched myself as I went over. The lookout had to look out! It was in the name! I was failing my task before it began.

The farther away I got from the mushrooms, the more my head cleared. By the time I reached the others, only night air and a cool mist greeted me.

Eddy took off his jacket, bundled it under his chin, and lay on his belly. Arish pulled his hood up and flopped onto his back, but Jo waited until I sat beside her before offering her lap as a pillow.

"It sorta smells like my shampoo out here," she said. "That's strange, right?"

Oh, thank goodness. Someone else had noticed. "I like it," said Eddy. "Makes me feel sleepy."

"You can't fall asleep!" Arish reached up a hand, like he could grab a star if he stretched high enough. "We gotta stay up. What kind of summer camp experience would this be otherwise?" He made a sound between a chuckle and a groan. "I've never been to any kind of camp before, let alone one with glowing trees. I gotta make this count."

I decided not to rain on his parade by pointing out we weren't sure what, specifically, glowed. Instead, I said, "Yeah, same here. It took ages to convince my mom to let me come, and only 'cause my dad felt guilty. Both of my parents are super strict."

Arish faced me. "Do they do the thing where they say, 'That wasn't done in my country'?" He deepened his voice, making the rest of us giggle.

I massaged the meat of my palm. "My dad does. He says he wasn't allowed to have sleepovers when he was growing up. A sleepaway camp is sort of a big deal." I adjusted my position. "They weren't like this with my big sister."

"Oh man, haven't heard any stories about her in ages," Jo said. "How is Pari, anyway?"

I didn't talk to my big sister often, but she'd called before I'd come to camp. Would she have heard the same music if she were here? Besides the usual night sounds, it was currently quiet. "She's good. Busy preparing the fields." To the others I added, "My sister is way, way older than me. She dropped out of college to live with a group of people on a farm in Iowa. My parents . . ." I switched palms to massage. Eddy and Arish watched me with wide eyes. "My parents weren't strict enough with her, they say. Like, my dad said he realized adopting American customs to raise her was a mistake, and my mom agreed. I think they're disappointed in her."

Dinner threatened to reappear in its half-digested form; I swallowed the sour taste back. I hoped they wouldn't be disappointed in *me*.

"And that's why you can't have sleepovers?" Eddy shook his head. "That's not fair. You're not the one who ran off to live on a farm. Not that there's anything wrong with that, but . . ."

"God," said Arish, "my parents would literally kill me if I did that. They're already not happy about my future stardom. Luckily, my two big sisters are gonna be doctors, and my older brother is gonna be an engineer, and the twins will be lawyers or something. There's so many of us, they'll probably forget about me, anyway."

"How many siblings do you have?" asked Jo.

"I'm kid four out of six. It's . . ." Arish's brows furrowed. He stacked his fists and placed his chin atop them. "It's a lot."

THE GLADE

No wonder he was the class clown. How else was anyone going to pay attention to him with so many kids at home?

"Do you have any siblings, Eddy-spaghetti?" he asked.

Eddy nodded. "A little sister, but she's four. Jo?"

"Just me." Jo leaned back on her hands, staring up. It was full night, stars blanketing the sky. They were brilliant out here, away from city pollution. "I live with my aunt and uncle," said Jo. "My dad died when I was a baby, and my mom . . ." She swallowed. I snuggled my face into her thigh instead of taking her hand or using our code words. "She's not around."

Jo didn't like talking about her mom, who'd been hospitalized when we were seven, about six months before we met. Most of what Jo'd told me about her was complicated. A mix of missing someone Jo didn't really know and being mad at her for being gone.

"That's rough," said Eddy with a sad smile. "My mom's not around either, but that's 'cause my parents divorced. We see her on weekends. Lately, we've been at my gramma's a lot since my dad got a new job and has to travel."

"Is that hard?" Knowing Jo, she was grateful he'd taken the attention off her.

Eddy picked at his pants. "Sorta. Gramma's awesome

and a great cook. It's better spending time with her than hearing my parents scream at each other. If they hate each other so much, how come they got married in the first place?"

"They must not have always hated each other," I said.

"Yeah, I guess. I just . . ." Eddy blew out a breath. "Sometimes I wonder whether—this is embarrassing." He looked away.

"We won't laugh," said Jo.

Eddy tapped his leg, then said in a rush, "I wonder why Ellie and I weren't enough. I mean, Ellie was a *baby* baby when they split. But me, I dunno. They didn't fight as much before she was born. Then she was, and it was like nothing I did was good enough to make up for having another kid around."

None of us said anything at first. Then Arish patted Eddy's shoulder, and Jo said, "I know how that feels. Not being good enough for them—the adults in your life."

I looked up into her face, but she was turned away. "Khoobee?" I asked.

She shrugged.

That was the second time tonight she hadn't said "mabuti" back.

THE GLADE

Normal night sounds filled our silence. The stars brightened overhead, twinkling. I yawned, then pinched my arm. "When do you think it'll start glowing?"

Arish tore a blade of grass. "It was pretty late when we saw it before. Probably past midnight."

Midnight! I bit back a groan. Only two full days at camp, and I was already exhausted. How were we going to stay up that late? How was *I* going to stay up that late?

A breeze rustled the leaves, but the noises from the branches sounded like creaking stairs. I stiffened and sat up. The hairs on the back of my neck rose. No eyes peeked at us from beyond the clearing, but I couldn't shake the feeling we were being watched.

Jo lay down, crossing her arms under her head like a pillow. Uncertain, I lay back down and cuddled her. It was chilly, and Jo was warm. I tucked my hands into my hoodie sleeves. Crickets chirped, and frogs croaked from somewhere farther away, a stream gurgling with them. Lightning bugs flickered above us, yellow green in their own glow, predicting what would happen later. I hoped.

I buried my face in Jo's shoulder. "If I had a phone," she said, "I could set an alarm. We could nap until midnight."

Mom and Dad said I could get a real phone (instead of the baby one that only let me call them and couldn't go online) at the end of seventh grade if I kept my grades up, but Jo's aunt and uncle said she couldn't get one until she got a job to pay for it.

"I don't have a phone anymore," said Eddy. "My parents keep fighting about letting me keep it."

"My mom wouldn't let me bring my phone. She said I'd break it," said Arish. "Man, parents are the worst."

Jo said nothing, and I scooched my face from her shoulder to the crook of her neck.

A moment later Arish said, "Oh shoot. Sorry, Jo."

"It's okay. Happens all the time." She cleared her throat. "There's probably no reception out here, anyway."

I couldn't tell if she was upset, and while I could use our code word again, I worried she'd brush it off a third time. But then she yawned and threw an arm around me, and I yawned back, and soon we were one big yawn fest.

"Hey," said Arish. "No sleeping! We gotta tell stories until the glow starts."

"Ugh." Eddy rolled over. "Fine, fine. What do you want to talk about?"

Arish launched into another one of his movie plots. I

smiled as he energetically explained the sequel to *The Spy Who Destroyed the Galaxy*. Eddy's responses came in and out of my awareness as my eyes shut.

Piiiiina, whispered the echoes in the forest. *Come down and play, Pina. . . .*

What the heck? My eyes flew open. Arish and Eddy were talking, and Jo was blinking sleepily, but it didn't look like any of them had heard the voice.

I rubbed my eyes. I had to stay awake. I was the strong, brave, nope-not-scared lookout tonight. I volunteered for the job! I had a lot to prove!

Piiiina, came the whispers again. *Time to sleep, Pina. . . .*

SIX

I found myself in a tiny, dark room. The smell of dirt filled my nostrils; the damp air crawled across my face and plugged my ears. I rubbed my eyes. Where was I? I'd been in the clearing, waiting for the glow and proving . . . something. I reached out, bumping into a soft wall. Feeling around and squinting (not that I could see any better), my fingers brushed something solid.

It felt like a . . . doorknob?

I turned it and pushed.

Light blared into my face. Blinking, I threw up my hands. When the brightness no longer seared my eyeballs, I looked around.

THE GLADE

I had to be dreaming.

The forest had transformed. A great mountain range crowned the horizon, but not of rocks—they were mushrooms, so large they would have towered above houses, like skyscrapers. Some had red caps and white spots, while others were brown and spotted like an egg. Instead of trees, giant reeds waved in the breeze, their feathered tops rubbing together with the sound of wind chimes. I wasn't on grass, either; I bent and ran my hands along the fuzzy green, orange, and blue patches of moss, or maybe lichen.

My hoodie stuck to my sweaty skin. I pulled it off and looped it around my waist, relishing the warmth that smelled like my parents' garden: like rain, like earth. Like my own personal heaven. I'd never had a dream this vivid before.

A butterfly flitted past me, then another. They weren't like any butterflies I'd seen before: bigger than my hand, with see-through wings of pale blue with black dots, and . . . were those teeth?

"Whoa!"

When I turned, Jo, Eddy, and Arish were behind me. Funny how dreams worked, with them popping up like daisies in the spring. I was glad I'd dreamt up my friends, though.

"Look at this place!" Eddy ran into an empty patch of lichen-moss grass, twirling around. Blue and orange powder puffed into the air. It smelled like peppermint. I sneezed.

"This is awesome!" said Jo. "It's like *Alice in Wonderland*!"

"'Oh, I've had such a curious dream!'" I quoted, because Jo didn't mind when I memorized parts of books and recited them to her.

Arish ran up to a bush. "Wow, look at this!" He plucked off a purple berry. "It smells like bubble gum!"

"Don't eat it! You don't know if it's safe!" Thinking about Alice reminded me of her misadventures. All we needed was for a Queen of Hearts to start shouting for our heads.

(Also, lots of berries were poisonous.)

Arish shrugged. "It's a dream, right?" He popped it into his mouth.

Was it? This was such a wondrous—and therefore unknown—world around us that it had to be a dream. I'd never had someone in my dreams tell me they were in one, though, like they were trying to remind me none of it was real.

THE GLADE

In the back of my mind, something nagged at me. I'd been talking before I'd fallen asleep; maybe that was it. Or maybe it was because plants could be dangerous, and my dream version of Arish wasn't listening to me, which was either my mind being very accurate or very mean.

He was chewing before I could protest again and blew a bubble. "Bubble berries!" he shouted when it popped over his face. He pulled off the remnants, laughing. "Look, there's another bush over there with pink ones!"

"Race you!" said Jo, because Jo loved racing, and I knew Jo better than the back of my hand. (Who spent time looking at the backs of their hands, anyway? I'd rather read a book.)

She rushed over, beating him, and tried a berry herself. "Whoa, it's, like, sour sweet. P, you'd love this. You gotta try it!"

What if we had to go to a dream doctor and there wasn't one around? Could I dream up urgent care if we got sick?

Typical. Everyone else was having fun while I was the worrywart.

Jo blew a bubble. As it grew to the size of her face, it turned white instead of pink before it detached and floated away like a helium balloon.

"Me next!" Eddy snatched his own berry off the bush. "Ohhh man, Pina, don't miss out! The rest of us feel fine!"

"C'mon, P!" Jo leapt into the air. In a single jump, she was back beside me. "It's just a dream. Kaya mo ba?"

Okay, clearly my mind was telling me to stop worrying. I'd conjured up my friends to keep me company in dreamland, and those dream friends wanted me to have fun.

"Khoobam." I accepted the offered berry from Jo. I rolled it between my fingers, careful not to squash it. It looked like a bright pink blackberry with extra-large drupelets.

"Go on," urged Dream Jo. "Try it."

I took a deep breath. A scientist had to experiment to get answers. Scientists couldn't let themselves get scared before trying. Before I could keep overthinking, I threw it in my mouth.

Sour burst on my tongue. The flavor was like pink lemonade but tarter, and as I chewed, I had the overwhelming urge to blow a bubble. Like Jo's, it broke off from my mouth and floated away.

It was delicious.

Of course we were safe in a dream. I didn't need to stand lookout for—

I gasped. Lookout! This was bad, very bad. I should have told the others to nudge me if I fell asleep before them. I pinched myself to wake up.

What had happened as I'd drifted off? Someone had called my name. Someone—or something.

The pinching wasn't working.

Arish threw himself into a fuzzy bush, then yelped and jumped out, rubbing his back. "Ow! That was sharp!"

On cue, a huge wasp the size of my head—no, bigger, the size of a cat—emerged from the bush, buzzing loud enough to rattle my teeth.

My mouth dried. I knew this was a bad idea! Why didn't anyone, including the people my mind made up, listen to me? We were bound to get a million wasp stings and have to go to a dream hospital and take ten million kinds of medicines with thirty thousand side effects!

I slapped my cheek. I needed to wake up five minutes ago.

But Arish, fearless as ever, said, "Don't even try it!" and threw a berry at the wasp to distract it. He jumped high in the air and kicked the striped abdomen. The wasp soared out of sight with a twinkle like we were in a TV show.

"I am a kung fu master!" Arish cackled. "Did you see that, Pina? I kicked its butt! I thought it would sting me, but *pow! Blam-o!* That sucker flew outta here!"

We were *so* lucky this was a dream. I lifted my arms over my head and tried to slow my breathing.

Relax, Piiinaaaaa, came a familiar voice. Once again no one else seemed to hear it.

"There's a three-headed moose by the river," yelled Eddy, who had climbed a nearby hill. "This place is awesome!"

"I wanna see!" Arish dashed over.

Maybe the voice—my brain?—was right. If giant wasps and three-headed moose were leaving us alone—assuming the wasp didn't find us again—this place probably wasn't so bad.

Jo summoned me to her latest bush examination. I jogged over and crouched to check it out. The smell of peppermint and strawberries smacked me in the face as I pushed aside blue leaves to reveal a red flower like a poinsettia but striped.

THE GLADE

"You can eat flowers, right?" asked Jo.

"Some kinds—"

She plucked off a petal and ate it. "Whoa! It tastes like candy canes but better!" She tore off the rest. "This is the coolest dream ever!"

Despite the fluttering in my belly, I tried a petal of my own. Dream Jo was right—it tasted like strawberries and cream with a hint of mint.

I couldn't help it: I laughed.

We picked more berries and flowers and headed to the boys. The green berries tasted like pomegranates but didn't blow bubbles; the ones with pink dots burst in our mouths like popping candy. But when we reached Arish and Eddy, they were staring off in the distance, concern on their faces.

Jo turned before I did. I gulped and did the same.

The hills were moving.

"Do you hear that?" Arish looked around. "Is that a music box?"

I squinted. No, those weren't hills. Everywhere else, the lichen-moss grass was orange or green or blue; those were black and brown—a mass of bumps moving toward us scary quick.

"What is that?" I asked.

My throat tightened. I wasn't sure I wanted to know the answer.

"I hear something," said Jo, eyebrows furrowed. "It sounds like . . ."

This was worse than the giant wasp or three-headed moose or butterfly with teeth. Dreams could become nightmares at any moment.

Why couldn't I force myself awake?

Come play, Piiiinaaaaaaa. . . .

The writhing group—not hills, but whatever covered them—propelled itself with what must have been legs. As thick as branches, the legs snapped out from the pile of whatever it was—nightmare fuel—before bending in precise angles and slamming down with a noise like crashing cymbals. The air shook with each step. More legs sprang up to drive the horde forward, and what felt like a gazillion eyes turned their attention on us.

Oh no.

Oh no oh no *oh no*.

And then I heard what the others did—the high whine of a little kid, the same kid telling me to sleep, asking me to play. (Not my brain, like I'd originally thought.)

THE GLADE

The itsy-bitsy spider went sneaking in the rain....

Those were the wrong words, but my mind shut down. My breath rang loud in my ears. I gulped, my throat desert dry, and gulped again. All I tasted was sand and the lingering odor of moldy fruit.

"I think," said Arish, "those are spiders."

Goose bumps rippled up my skin. I swayed, light-headed.

Eddy shifted his weight. "That's a lot of spiders."

What else could I have dreamt but those beady eyes? Those legs covered in sticky, wiry hairs? What else would have haunted my sleep but spiders of every shape and size?

Little did it know ... there would be a lot of pain....

A floating sensation washed over me. This was it. There was no way I could survive a spider army. If I'd done my job as lookout, none of this would have happened because I wouldn't have fallen asleep. "We're going to die," I said, sounding a lot calmer than I felt.

"We are *not* going to die," Jo and Arish said together.

"We're dreaming." Eddy placed a hand on my arm, bringing my foggy mind back to earth. His voice shook. "None of this is real. C'mon, Pina. Breathe."

I *was* breathing! In fact, I was breathing so fast, my

head was dizzy. Spots popped across my vision. All I could do was breathe and watch the waves of spiders and smell the stink of my fear like spoiled milk.

Nausea gripped my belly. My worst nightmares had found me. If this weren't a dream with made-up plants, I'd try to calm myself by naming them, but nope! It was a make-believe world about to kill me.

My vision dimmed, then brightened as the spiders closest to us bared their red bellies. The larger spiders were drawing nearer, smelling like garbage left out in the sun for too long.

If it had known . . . it might have gone inside. . . .

"We're gonna die!" I screamed, latching onto Jo's arm for dear life. Even in my dreams I had to reach for her. Who was I kidding? Of course I couldn't do anything on my own. Jo had to protect me, like always.

But it was Eddy who stepped in front of us, puffing out his chest. "We are *not going to die!*"

He began to glow.

Gold light shone from Eddy as he levitated above us, his clothes morphing into armor, broadening across his chest and clamping around his legs. A cape flared out behind him as a giant staff appeared in his hand. His hair grew into a cloud-like puff, a crown threaded through, and when the light cleared, two unicorns with their horns crossed were etched into his chest plate.

For a moment, the creepy child's slow singing was replaced with the *Unicorn Quest* theme music.

"A magical girl transformation," said Jo, awestruck.

Eddy had turned into a magical superhero to save us!

But the itsy-bitsy spider . . .

Curled on . . .

Its side . . .

And died.

A giant leg crashed down beside us. Arish yelled and dashed forward, shoving me out of the way before he also transformed. His clothes altered into a sleek space suit, red gloves sliding into place with a ray gun in one hand. His signature glasses fell over his eyes, and he aimed, shooting lasers. "Heck yeah! A built-in computer!" He pressed a finger to the earpiece he now wore. "Aim for the bellies or cut down the legs! Those are the weak spots. I'll get the eyes!"

Did Arish have his own music too, or was I imagining the *Operation Possible* theme?

Jo grinned and cracked her knuckles. "My turn!" She

let out a crowing howl and charged at the nearest spider bunch, transforming into a ferocious shelled bear from *DynoHunters*.

It was kind of cool that I could dream my friends becoming heroes to save me.

Silly Pina, whispered the kid's voice. *Can't save yourself, even in a dream.*

Only I was left standing defenseless. Of course I'd be the one unable to help. Silly, useless Pina. I wanted to curl up in a ball and cry. The voice, wherever it came from, was right.

But . . . was I defenseless and useless? This was *my* dream, after all. If I could give my friends superpowers, why couldn't I also give them to myself? Why couldn't I also fight my biggest fear? The fear that filled my nostrils with a smell like Mom's compost bucket: overripe fruit, decaying leaves.

I shut my eyes.

Silly Pina, scared of spiders, sang the voice.

I gritted my teeth and tuned it out. Picturing things didn't happen with my brain, but I could tell myself stories as if I were reading.

My favorite book heroes always faced their fears eventually, especially when the people they cared about were at stake. I wasn't sure that I could be tough like them, but there had to be *some*thing I could do to help.

Dream or no dream, I couldn't watch my friends get hurt and do nothing about it.

My skin tingled, zapping me like static electricity. When I opened my eyes, I held a stem with long, oval-shaped leaves, ending in tiny purple flower buds. I'd recognize that calming smell anywhere. *Lavandula*—lavender.

Of course!

My friends continued to grapple with the spiders. I yelped as one charged me, but Jo roared and swiped it out of my way with her giant paw. Eddy hovered above me, spinning his staff and firing magical bolts of light. I concentrated on creating a bushy barrier around me and Arish, who was shooting sight-destroying lasers between shouting instructions.

"What are you doing?" he yelled. "Get to safety!"

"I'm not leaving you!" I might not have felt brave enough to start the fight, but this—creating a safety zone—was playing defense. Something only I could do. "Jo, Eddy, watch out!"

A particularly large spider reared. Jo copied the motion with a snarl, and I begged my dreams to protect her like she was protecting me. Lavender and marigolds and mint exploded from the ground around her, and the spider rolled back, belly-up, in its haste to escape. Eddy, floating nearby, finished charging his spell to blast a hole in the beast, which vanished in a puff of purple smoke.

It was working. We were doing it!

Together, we beat the spiders back. Arish shouted tips from within our safety zone as he shot his laser gun. Eddy blasted magic from his staff. Jo bulldozed anyone who came near us.

And me? I grew thick hedges to manage the attacking horde.

One giant spider remained, this one the largest. My plants popped up to discombobulate the creature. As it stumbled, Arish took out a few of the eyes, which let Eddy shoot its limbs before Jo tackled it to the ground.

Smoke billowed over the field as the final spider disappeared. I caught my breath, my arms wobbly like spaghetti. (Why did my *arms* hurt?) The smoke twisted in the sky, making a shape like a floating skull, then a skull with eight legs, before dissipating.

"Is it over?" Arish pulled his glasses off. "Did we win?"

"Holy cannoli." Eddy settled back on the ground and wiped his face with his cape. "I think we did it. We won."

"We did it!" Jo shrank back into a human and threw her arms around me. I laughed and danced with her in a circle. "We kicked spider butt!"

Arish jumped in to join the hug, and the three of us pulled in Eddy too. "What the heck was up with the plants?" asked Arish.

I beamed. "Spiders don't like the oils in strong-smelling plants. They avoid them."

"Leave it to your big brain to figure that out!" Jo cheered again, pumping her fist. "We'd have saved you, but you protected us!"

"Three cheers for Pina!" said Arish.

"Three cheers for all of us!" I said.

We huddled together, laughing and shouting over one another to relive the best parts of the battle.

But in the back of my mind, I knew things couldn't be this easy. I'd abandoned my post and fallen asleep, and when I woke up, there might be a lot of trouble to pay.

And I couldn't help but strain my ears, as if I could still hear the kid singing.

SEVEN

A streak of sunlight slithered across my face as I woke. My neck ached. I reached to rub it and groaned as my back cracked, and I groaned more when the soreness in my thighs hit. It felt like ants ran up and down one arm.

Oh—I was on a bed of grass. Where . . . ?

The clearing in the middle of the woods!

No wonder my body hurt; I'd cut off the circulation in my arm when I used it as a pillow, and the ground wasn't exactly a mattress. Jo was tucked beside me, Eddy was curled in a ball, and Arish was sprawled out, his mouth open in a snore.

Urgency boiled inside me, but I didn't know why. From my dream? What *had* I dreamed?

Wait—dreamed? Had we slept through the glow? I was supposed to watch out for us! Shoot! I sat up, squinting at the sky as it lightened with oranges and pinks. Early enough, but people would be up soon. We needed to get back to the cabins before anyone noticed we were gone.

At the corner of my vision flickered transparent blue wings, a flash of teeth. I rubbed my eyes, but it was gone.

That seemed familiar. . . .

At the edge of the clearing, I could have sworn the mushrooms pulsed orange. I could have sworn someone whispered my name. My head swam; I shut my eyes until the feeling passed. Bits and pieces of my dream returned to me. It had been super vivid, with the four of us in it— what had happened? Why had I felt so desperate? Chewing gum, something about spiders?

I shuddered.

When my head cleared, I woke the others. Jo buried her face against me as Eddy looked dazed. Arish inhaled so sharply that he sat up, arms shooting out in the middle of a karate move. His brain seemed to catch up with him a moment later, since he put his arms down and smiled sheepishly.

"I had the wildest dream." Jo rubbed her face.

"Same," said Arish. "I think it was some high-stakes action dream! My heart's racing!"

"Let's talk about it later." The time worried me. If only I wore a watch! "We have to get back before anyone notices we're gone." I'd royally messed up, and I had to make it better. Maybe then my body would calm down.

"Did you see that?" interrupted Eddy.

Arish yawned. "See what?"

"I thought I saw . . . never mind. Pina's right. Let's go."

Forest sounds surrounded us: rustling bushes, scuttling animals, singing birds. Everything seemed overly normal—no music, no smells, just (loud) nature. Each noise sent a jolt down my spine. What if we got caught? What would happen to us? I shushed the others.

And it was a good thing I did, because I could hear a voice as we got closer to the cabins. Jo tiptoed ahead to get a look at what we were dealing with before hurrying back. "It's Ms. Angela!"

My stomach churned. We were caught. We were so dead. Never again would Mom let me—

THE GLADE

Jo grabbed my shoulders and shook me. "Stay with us, Pina. We need a plan."

Sweat shone on Eddy's forehead. Arish covered his mouth like he was going to be sick. Both turned to me with panic on their faces.

I dug my nails into my palms. Focus, Pina! I inched over until I could peer out of the forest.

Ms. Angela's shock of red hair tumbled down her shoulders. She paced, gesturing with her hands and ranting. She tugged on her hair like she was annoyed, and I saw an earpiece; she was on the phone. Behind her was a cabin with a gated garden. Rather than walk toward the main camp, we'd gone to the edges, straight to where Ms. Angela stayed!

I took quick stock of our surroundings. If I were a hero in a book, I knew what I'd do. "Okay," I said to the others. "On three, you two run to that cluster of trees, and Jo will hide behind that big one over there. Arish, can you do a birdcall?"

"What do you take me for, an amateur?"

I nodded, my mind working fast. "Right. When the three of you are in position, chirp or whatever as the signal. I'll distract her. When she goes to check, we make a break for it. Got it?"

Arish gulped and nodded. Eddy looked determined, but Jo looked worried. "Are you sure this will work?" she asked.

"Yup." For the others' sake, I had to sound confident. Inside, I was a nervous wreck. "On three. One, two . . . three!"

The others ran. I gathered big rocks and twigs. Breathing hard, I gripped the twigs and waited. I could see Ms. Angela from where I stood. I couldn't hear what she was saying, but she sounded angry.

A twitter sounded. (Arish's signal didn't sound nearly as real as he thought it did.) Ms. Angela turned. That's when I moved, snapping the twigs and tossing the rocks as far away from me as I could.

I sprinted to Jo behind the big tree as the boys dashed away. Ms. Angela went to investigate—my plan had worked! Jo grabbed my hand, and we ran as fast as we could to our cabin.

I'd done it. I'd been brave by myself and protected my friends.

Why . . . did it feel like this hadn't been the first time?

We slid inside the screen door, barely catching it before it slammed shut. Shuffling came from inside. Counselors were up!

THE GLADE

I yanked Jo into the bathroom. We huddled in a stall. Flip-flops slapped against the floor, and a sink turned on. I shut my eyes, hoping they wouldn't see our four feet, and covered my mouth to muffle my breathing. After everything, were we going to be caught so close to our beds?

But then the sink turned off, and the person yawned, heading out. After another few moments, we emerged from the bathroom. Whoever it had been was back in bed.

Relief ballooned in my chest.

Passing by Constance and Mackenzie and Kiki, I felt guilty that we'd had this adventure without them. Should we have told them what we'd been planning? Would they have wanted to come along? But the clearing in the woods was *our* thing, mine and Jo's and Eddy's and Arish's, and it felt wrong to invite others.

For the first time, I had a group of friends.

Based on the wall clock, we had an hour before we had to be up. I collapsed on my bed and passed out.

Before the boys could find us for breakfast, Kiki beckoned me and Jo over to sit with them, Constance, and Mackenzie. Rain clouded the skies. The dank camp smell was back, but I was getting used to it. Jo and I were both too sleepy to be chatty, but the other three kept up conversation until Mackenzie snapped her fingers in front of our faces after repeating a question for the third time.

"Sorry." I yawned.

She crossed her arms. "What is with you two today?"

"Didn't sleep well," I said.

"I had the weirdest dream," said Jo. "And I keep thinking I'm seeing things."

"What kind of things?" asked Kiki.

"Stuff that happened in the dream. Like, I thought I saw giant mushrooms when I woke up! How weird is that? Or—or I thought at first the bushes outside weren't green but blue. You were in the dream, P, and so were Eddy and Arish, and we were running around eating . . . berries? And I think I became a bear at some point?"

Alarm bells rang in my brain, but I couldn't figure out why. Jo's dream sounded silly—so what? Yet my mind screamed at me to pay attention to something she'd said.

Jo had seen—or thought she'd seen—giant mushrooms when she woke up. A leftover from her dream. Hadn't I also thought I'd seen something weird? Did those dream "glitches" mean something? Could they explain the frantic energy thrumming through me as I'd woken?

"Wish I turned into a bear in my dream," said Constance gloomily. "I had the *I didn't do a big class assignment and it's due today* dream again."

Since it was raining, we stayed inside to play a board game. Before long I was laughing alongside the others, distracted by dice rolls and loud groans and Mackenzie's cheers whenever she made a good move.

The rain let up about an hour before lunch, and Kiki suggested Red Rover, which Jo loved. The counselors were game, although Bethany complained to her minions (to no one's surprise). The other campers seemed excited, though, so we dashed outside. The air smelled like rain, washing away the building's smell, and I inhaled deeply as I admired the giant mushrooms soaring in the background.

Wait. What?

I blinked when my brain registered what I was seeing. There were no mushrooms—just black spruce trees reaching into the sky. Gosh, that dream was messing with me.

It . . . had been a dream, hadn't it?

We squared off in teams, alternating on calling names. A couple of campers didn't break through the linked arms, but Jo and Kiki did, and, surprising for someone her size, so did Constance.

"Red Rover, Red Rover, send Pina on over!"

Okay. I could do this. I looked at the joined hands until I found two smaller kids, a place to break the chain. I dashed.

But, just my luck, two things happened at the same time: my foot slipped on the soft ground and someone called my name.

Instead of breaking through the linked arms, I face-planted in the mud. My whole shirt was covered as I pushed up, spitting and scooting away onto grass. If anyone *had* said my name, it was as a distraction.

Giggles erupted behind me. My breath hiccupped as my chest tightened. This was school all over again, with the Joseph Collins crew taunting me for sucking at PE. Tears stung my eyes.

Except no one, not even the laughing kids, said anything mean. Kiki actually asked if I was okay and tried to rub the mud off my face with a large leaf. That made me laugh a little, since it was such a silly plan and I knew they were only trying to help.

Jo was staring off in the distance, eyes glassy.

"Khoobee?" I asked.

"Yeah, mabuti. I feel like I've been seeing—whatever. Whoa, you're covered! Did you fall? That sucks." Grimacing, she squatted to rub mud off my cheeks. "Your mom's gonna kill you if you don't get that mud out. You want company to change?"

"Nah, it's okay." Lunch would be soon. Food would make us both feel better.

But when Jo helped me up, my knee buckled. I yelped as it slammed to the ground, pain shooting up my leg. Gingerly, I sat back down and stuck my leg out. My knee had a large scrape underneath the dirt, and my ankle was beginning to swell.

Great.

Jo dropped back down beside me. "Shoot! Is it bad?"

"It's okay," I managed. "Startled me, mostly."

One of the counselors hurried over. They paled and covered their mouth. "Ugh, I can't do blood." (There wasn't that much.) "Molly, can you take her to Angela?"

"I'll do it!" came a chipper voice. To my surprise, Bethany skipped over. "I know where Ms. Angela's cabin is!"

"Thank you, Bethany, but one of us has to go with her anyway." Counselor Molly helped me up. Bethany pouted but didn't argue. Jo stepped forward to join, but I told her I'd see her at lunch. I could get first aid by myself; I didn't want to take her away from the game.

Limping and trying not to get the counselor muddy, I leaned on Molly as we made our slow way to Ms. Angela's cabin. I hadn't gotten a great look at it this morning, and since I wasn't trying to be sneaky this time, I could admire the cute log building with its wooden fence. A gate with a detailed metal arch marked where the stone walkway split, one path leading to the door, the other to the garden. I itched to head over and check it out, but my knee and ankle had other opinions.

Inside, the icky smell returned with a vengeance. I wrinkled my nose. Molly told me to sit tight and went searching for a towel.

"Pina? Is that you?"

Balancing against the wall, I took my shoes off and hopped into the living room. Eddy sat on the couch. He jerked up, his arm bent and clutched to his belly. "What happened?"

"Tripped during Red Rover. You?"

"Tripped during archery." He grimaced. "It's been a weird day."

THE GLADE

"Tell me about it."

Molly came back with a couple of towels, laying the big one on a folding chair, and said Ms. Angela would be out when her phone call was over. After she left, I wiped my face with the damp hand towel and asked Eddy about Bombshell, since the glittery unicorn wasn't with him.

"She's with Arish. I . . ." Eddy exhaled and rubbed the back of his neck with his good hand before lowering his voice. "I think sleeping outside messed with me."

In my chair, I bent to remove my muddy socks and used the final towel to clean my legs and arms. "How come?"

He shook his head. "It's silly."

"I won't laugh."

He stared at his hands. "I've been seeing things out the corner of my eye. First it was weird-colored bushes, but then I saw a moose behind the archery range."

Seeing things . . . like the butterfly with teeth or mushroom trees?

"A moose?"

"With three heads."

"That's . . . yeah, okay. I get why you didn't want to share. But I believe you." The place behind my eyes ached. I massaged my forehead. The alarm bells from breakfast picked up their ringing in my head. "I've been seeing things too. I only tripped 'cause I thought I heard my name. Okay, that sounds normal, but—but it wasn't a voice I knew."

"Ugh. This is bizarro."

As we both fell silent, I looked around, curious how Ms. Angela had set up her space. The living room had the couch Eddy was on, plus an armchair facing a giant TV. Across from us was a small kitchen with shiny appliances. Everything looked brand new, like a furniture store setup. If it wasn't for the usual camp funk (and knowing better), I'd have thought no one lived here.

Then I noticed the bookshelf. Unable to help myself, I hobbled over to read the titles. "I guess Ms. Angela is into mushrooms."

Eddy got up to join me. "How do you know?"

I pointed. "These are books on mycology." I pulled one out and paged through until I got to a diagram of mycelium networks. "Oh, these are really cool! So mushrooms are like the fruit of a fungus. They release spores, which are like fungus seeds. But the majority of the fungus is underground in what's called mycelium. Scientists are still studying everything mycelium does, since it's pretty important to how plants can communicate with one another, especially trees, but they're also important for nutrient gathering!"

I flipped more pages. "My favorite fact is that mycelium can grow huge! With all the mushrooms I've seen, I bet there are giant fungal systems around here." I stopped myself from rambling further. "Sorry. That was probably boring." I waited for the usual eye roll or zoned-out face as I returned the book.

Eddy shook his head. "It wasn't. It's pretty cool how much you know about plants!"

My chest warmed. I didn't bother to tell him fungi weren't plants. "Thanks. People don't usually think so. Even Jo gets bored."

"Huh. That doesn't seem like them."

I shrugged.

"What about your other friends?"

I cleared my throat and hopped back to my seat. "I, um. Don't really have a lot of other friends. There are classmates I like, but we don't hang out."

Eddy shot me a sad smile. "I get it. After my parents divorced, we had to move, and I started a new school. It was hard to make friends when my classmates have known one another for so long."

"It sounds like the divorce was hard."

"It was. I mean, it's better than having them constantly fighting. But sometimes . . ." He swallowed. I smiled a little and nodded, so he continued. "At first I hoped they'd get back together. Eventually it was obvious how much better things are this way. But sometimes, when it's just me and Ellie and Gramma, I miss having everyone together."

"I'm sorry." I wasn't sure what else to say. "That sounds lonely."

His eyes flicked away. "Yeah." Then his expression focused. "Oh, hey, look at this. I think it's Ms. Angela."

I shifted to see what he was looking at. He crossed into the kitchen and picked up a framed photograph. A teenager was bent over, hugging a kid while the kid laughed, their gap teeth on display. The teen was definitely Ms. Angela, with the same red locks (but no glasses). The kid looked a lot like her.

"It could be her little sibling," said Eddy. "They look alike, don't they?"

"Same face," I agreed. "Is that the Rec Hall behind them?"

THE GLADE

"Huh." Eddy leaned closer to the picture. "It looks like it, yeah. Didn't she say she was a camper before the camp shut down? Maybe they were both campers. She looks more like a counselor here, though."

"Finally!" came a yell from the office. Eddy returned the photo, and we hurried back to our seats. A door down the hall opened. "I am so sorry that took so long," said Ms. Angela as she emerged. "Doctor calls always do. George and Molly said neither of you were hurt too bad?"

"A sprain," said Eddy. "Pina looks pretty bad, though."

"It's the mud," I said.

"Let's get you two patched up and to lunch before it's over." Ms. Angela pulled out a first aid kit from under the sink and joined us in the living room. She gave Eddy a sling and an ice pack, and after cleaning and bandaging my knee, she had me wear my muddy sock so the ice pack could nestle between it and my shoe. "No more physical activities for the rest of the day for either of you. Your bodies need to rest. I'll—"

A ringtone floated toward us. Ms. Angela muttered under her breath. "I'm sorry, I have to get that. Hurry on to lunch."

Eddy helped me limp outside. The humidity blasted

us. "Do you want to change?" asked Eddy. "I can help you to your cabin."

That was nice of him to offer, so I agreed.

When we reached the girls' cabin, I heard a noise from somewhere behind us, sounding like an old marker squeaking against a whiteboard. I glanced over my shoulder.

"What is it?" asked Eddy.

"Thought I heard something. Never mind."

We headed inside. A chill raced up my arms when the screen door slammed behind us. My teeth clacked as I guided Eddy toward my bunk.

"Why is it so cold?" Eddy shivered.

"I thought it was just me." Together, Eddy and I pulled out my suitcase so I could get a change of clothes. "It's probably nothing. Be right back."

I limped to the front of the cabin. Footsteps chased after me, but when I spun around, no one was there. Hopping into the bathroom, I yanked the curtain closed in one of the shower stalls, my heart knocking against my ribs. Sweat beaded on my upper lip as I held my breath.

Nothing happened. Sheesh, what was I expecting? Eddy couldn't pull a prank from across the big room. Sleeping outside had probably messed with me, too.

THE GLADE

On the other hand, I'd been hearing things since yesterday.

After washing up and changing into new clothes—shoving the muddy ones into a plastic bag to rinse later—I heard the scratching noise again, this time from the cabin roof. I winced, rubbing my ear like someone was tapping my eardrum. Were the ceiling fans rattling more than usual? They were kept on and made noises, but the scratching was new.

"That's it." I readjusted the ice pack at my ankle. "Eddy, if you're doing that, cut it out!"

A long pause, then: "I thought it was you."

"What?"

Eddy met me halfway back to my bed, his face peaky. "The scratching?"

"Could be a branch."

"None of the trees hang over the roof."

We looked at each other for a long minute before Eddy deposited my dirty-clothes bag onto my bed.

Then we checked outside.

A spider the size of a school bus arched a giant leg over the log walls, scraping the Virginia creeper vines growing there. Most of its body settled on the roof. Each individual black hair, the length of my arm, danced in the breeze. Its eyes had a blue sheen. Worst of all were the brown and gray mushrooms covering its back like pus-filled boils ready to pop. And the smell—the stench of old fish.

That . . . *monster* had been on top of our heads the whole time!

My throat seized. Air stuttered in my lungs. My chest was going to burst. I took one shaking step back, then another, my knee buckling as I put too much weight on my swollen ankle.

"Uh . . . Pina . . ."

Those beady eyes turned to us.

"Run!" I screamed.

Eddy zigzagged across the grass, and I hopped on one leg, trying to keep up, before I went flying. My hands sprawled out to break my fall, and I landed hard on my wrists. Wincing, I rolled over, shielding my face from the impending attack.

Nothing happened.

Nothing was chasing us.

I rubbed my red palms, brushing off wet grass and a tangle of vines. "Pina!" gasped Eddy, collapsing beside me. "Are you okay?"

THE GLADE

"Yeah." I sat up. "Did you . . . ?"

Eddy gulped. "See a spider the size of a truck?"

How was this possible? The largest spider species in the world was no bigger than a dinner plate. (I looked it up to fight my fear with research, but it made it worse.) And they definitely didn't have mushrooms growing out of them. My overactive imagination would have been the culprit if Eddy hadn't also seen it, since I'd been dreaming of spiders since coming to camp.

Including last night.

The details flooded back: the berries, the bubbles, the spiders, the transformations. From the little she'd said at breakfast, Jo had dreamt those too.

And like Jo, Eddy and I had been seeing things all morning. What about Arish?

"Did you dream last night?" I could hear my own urgency.

Eddy cocked his head. "Yeah, why?"

I gestured to where the spider had been. "Eating berries, fighting giant spiders?"

He gaped at me. "How did you know?"

I knew it—he *did* have the same dream!

"*There* you two are!"

We looked over to see Arish and Jo headed toward us. "We've been looking everywhere for you," said Jo. "Lunch ended ten minutes ago."

"Plus," added Arish, "we're about two seconds away from being chucked into the loony bin."

Jo stiffened. Her mom had also been "chucked into the loony bin," and since I'd learned this, I'd also learned that a lot of insults make fun of disabilities.

I didn't want to force Jo to share something so personal, and I was a little nervous that Arish might be mad at me for saying something. Was there a way to ask him not to say those things without hurting his feelings? Did it make sense to protect him when Jo was the one affected?

As usual, Jo beat me to it. "That's not nice. Don't say things like that. Why are you on the ground? You okay?"

Arish blinked and opened his mouth, but nothing came out.

Eddy said, "We were chased by a giant spider."

"You *what*?"

The other two joined us on the grass. As Eddy explained what we'd seen, I pondered. Had we, all four of us, shared a dream last night?

It shouldn't have been possible. Sometimes people saw

THE GLADE

things and doctors got worried, but this was different. Eddy and I, and probably Jo, had seen the *same* things, had the *same* dream. How many people had shared dreams before? Were we a science experiment in the making?

"After you left," Arish said to Eddy, "I saw a giant killer wasp about to sting—uh, I forget their name. But I saw dancing mushrooms too! At least I thought I did. But so did Jo! Right?"

"Dancing mushrooms and striped flowers," she confirmed. It seemed like both she and Arish were past his "loony bin" comment.

"If we hadn't been chased by a spider big enough to cover the roof, I'd think you were pulling my leg," said Eddy. "But Pina and I both saw it."

"None of this makes sense!" said Arish. "How can we all see things that aren't there?"

"Jo, help me up." I reached for her. She yanked me a little hard. I winced but kept a hand on her shoulder to steady myself. "I have a hypothesis."

"What's your hi-poe-thee-sis, Detective P?" Jo, exaggerating the word, held up an invisible magnifying glass. "Actually, it should be Scientist P! What are scientists called?"

I grinned at her antics, nudging her toward the cafeteria. "I think 'doctors' since most have PhDs. Anyway, we've been seeing things today that shouldn't exist in our world. But we've seen them before."

"What do you mean?" asked Arish.

"Do you remember your dreams from last night? Where we were running in a colorful field and eating berries? And fighting an army of spiders?"

Arish and Jo both looked surprised. "How did you know about the spiders?" asked Jo. "I didn't tell you about that."

"You dreamt that too?" asked Arish. "It was awesome. Eddy turned into the coolest warrior princess."

Eddy beamed. "And Jo, they became a turtle-bear!" He gave Jo a warm smile. My stomach clenched into a rock. Ugh. I hated that my body reacted to my feelings.

Jo's hair was too short to tuck behind her ear, but she tried anyway, her other hand steadying me. "Oh, I dunno. Pina was able to control those plants. That's a lot cooler than a Dyno."

Yeah, it was cool, maybe (okay, not the plant thing; that was the least interesting transformation), but it was also scary. Dream or no dream, we'd been in danger—if not during, then definitely when Ms. Angela nearly caught us. And I kept replaying the eerie singing, a voice the others hadn't heard until the end.

"I think we had the same dream," I explained. "We shared it, somehow. Maybe it was the berries? Wait, no, we didn't eat those until we were already asleep. But a shared dream is the only logical explanation for why we're seeing things from it. The question is, how did it happen? And why are we seeing them while we're awake? It's freaky."

Jo shrugged. "I guess so."

"I think it's cool!" said Arish. "How do you think it happened?"

"I'm not sure," I admitted. "Something about where we fell asleep, maybe. Plants can have wild effects on your brain. Usually that's when you eat them, but maybe one makes a kind of oil that does the same thing?"

"Hmm." Eddy frowned. "I think we should tell George. Remember how he found us that first night? I think he knows a lot more than he said about the glow and this whole camp."

"He did toss the whole Minnesota Nice thing out the window that night." Arish rubbed his chin in contemplation. "And he almost had a meltdown when we were telling stories at the Big Weenie Roast. He grew up around here. He probably does know more."

I didn't like it. "Won't we get into trouble? He said we shouldn't go into the woods alone."

"There's not *technically* a rule about it," said Arish. "Eddy checked the counselor handbook in the cabins."

"Shouldn't we try Bethany first?" My voice held little conviction. "She's George's little sister."

Jo groaned. "Ugh. She's so mean. She'd probably laugh at us."

"We wouldn't risk getting in trouble with her," I pointed out.

"But what would we say?" asked Eddy. "George has already seen the glow. Bethany might know more about the old camp or the missing kid, but wouldn't she have shared that at the campfire?"

"That's a good point," said Jo. My insides balled like I was going to be sick. Why wasn't she taking my side? "Besides, with how much she loves rules and Ms. Angela and bossing people around, she probably would get us in trouble."

"Aww, don't worry, Pina." Arish came over to my other side to support me as Jo tied her shoelaces. "What's

THE GLADE

George gonna do? If he tattles, he'll have to admit he wasn't watching us when he should have been."

That was not as reassuring as he seemed to think it was.

"Speaking of Ms. Angela," said Eddy, "that was so cool this morning, Pina. You saved our butts! She was nice to us in the cabin, so it must have worked."

"Oh yeah!" said Arish. "We would have been goners without our pro lookout!"

Jo beamed at me. "I knew you could do it."

My cheeks warmed. "Thanks. I'm glad we didn't get caught." Which was why going to George seemed like a bad idea. Arish declared that I'd get us out of any sticky situation, and the others agreed. I wished I felt as confident as they did.

EIGHT

Even though lunch was technically over, some campers and counselors were hanging out. Arish was ready to charge George while Eddy and I got food, but I convinced him to wait. No longer hungry, I picked at my plate, my mind whirling through possibilities that could implode in our faces and ruin camp and destroy any chance of becoming Pina 2.0 and—

Knuckles rapped on my head. "Earth to Pina. Kaya mo ba?" Reading my expression, Jo wrapped an arm around me and squeezed. "It's gonna be okay. I'll fight George if I gotta."

Good thing I wasn't drinking anything, or I would

have snorted it. Jo always knew how to make me feel better.

Since George was on cleanup duty, we waited until the remainder of the camp headed outside to approach him. "You look like the cat who ate the canary," he accused. "What have you guys done this time?"

"Nothing!" Arish held up his hands. "We have a few questions you might be able to answer."

"About the glow," added Eddy. "And the clearing that gives you intense dreams."

George froze. Oh, he for sure knew something.

"Good grief, didn't I tell you not to go into the woods at night?" He tapped his foot, *taptaptap*. "A kid went missing in there, dontcha know."

"The one from the campfire story?" I asked.

"You got that right. We tell that story to talk about outdoor safety."

"You mean that whole thing with you and Bethany was staged?" Arish threw up his hands. "That was some acting!"

"That's not what I meant," said George. "Outside of Scout circles, it's more like a local legend. Bethany was sharing to scare, not teach."

"So what's the *real* story?" asked Eddy.

George sighed. "The deal is: a kid walked into the woods and was found unconscious, and the camp shut down." He brightened. "That's why I became an Eagle Scout."

"A what?" I asked.

George held up his wrist to reveal a watch on a leather band. On the watch face, a red, white, and blue banner read BE PREPARED, hanging above a metallic eagle with USA printed across it. "An Eagle Scout," he repeated. "Once I learned the truth, I thought, heck, I need to make sure it doesn't happen to another kid!" He puffed out his chest, looking a little like a turkey.

"You think the kid went to the clearing?" asked Jo. "Nothing bad happened to us when we were there."

Except for the giant spider army and creepy singing and almost getting caught by Ms. Angela.

Eddy rubbed his arm in the sling. "Except for the visions today."

And that.

George raised both eyebrows. "Visions?"

We explained what we'd done. As we talked, George's expression grew more and more tired until he sat down.

THE GLADE

"Uff-da. You're not imagining things. You went to the Glade."

The hushed name sent a shiver down my spine. I grabbed Jo's arm without looking.

"Old farts in the area say the outdoors round these parts are alive," continued George, "beyond what's natural. Local legend goes, if you spend too long in these here woods, you'll never be seen again. There're stories of hikers gone missing. Some say bigfoot took 'em, but a few talk about the Glade."

There was that name again.

"Not many people know about it," he added. "Those that do say it's a portal to another world, but that if you go in, you don't come back, or if you do come back, you're not the same. I thought it was just stories until I discovered it myself, far as that goes." George fingered his—yup, orange—lanyard, which ended in a bundle of keys, before rising to continue sweeping. "Have you heard of lucid dreaming?"

We shook our heads.

George slid over a bucket of soapy water and shoved a wet rag into Arish's hand. "I don't want to put you out, but the help would be appreciated." To the rest of us, he said, "You know when you're in a dream and realize you're dreaming?"

"That happens to me sometimes," said Eddy, wiping down tables with Arish. "Usually in the middle of a nightmare. It's like my mind remembers it's a dream, so it's not as scary."

Guess he didn't think nightmares were for babies anymore. I wish that happened when *I* got nightmares.

Jo stoppered and filled one of the sinks with water and dish soap. After she pulled over a chair for me, I grabbed a towel to dry her washed dishes. "So this Glade place," Jo said, elbow-deep in soapy water, "is what makes you wake up inside your dreams? I knew I was dreaming last night. And we could control what was happening a little bit."

"You bet." George grabbed a dustpan.

"How does that work?" I wished I'd read about the science of dreams, but medical stuff wasn't as interesting to me as other sciences. "What causes it?"

George shrugged, to my disappointment. "No clue. It's not consistent each time, far as I can tell. The first time I slept in the Glade, I didn't remember my dreams."

"We didn't when we woke up, either." I dried the

dishes that Jo piled in the empty sink. "Maybe something about a bunch of us sleeping there together helped us remember. Have you tried staying there with friends, George?"

George's whole face and ears and neck turned red. "I've never gone with anyone else."

Oh. I felt bad for him. I knew what it was like not to have a lot of friends, but at least I had Jo.

"But I did tell someone about it once," he said quickly. "Chris Heaney. I thought . . . well, a guy coulda thought we were friendly if he wasn't careful."

George's face clouded, and though his lips trembled and he blinked rapidly, he didn't seem angry—he seemed heartbroken.

"What happened?" I hoped I sounded gentle.

The apple in George's throat bobbed. "I told him about the clearing, and he said he'd check it out. After, he stopped talking to me, like I'd cussed his mama. It was like he wasn't the same person. He had this blank look in his eyes whenever I saw him from then on."

Poor George. It sucked that his only friend had abandoned him.

Interesting, though, that the five of us had something

like that in common. Eddy missed his parents. Arish didn't say it, but six kids were a lot, like he was one of too many. And me and Jo only had each other. Did the Glade call to lonely kids? Could it sense us?

"Wait, you said you didn't remember your *first* dream," said Arish before it got awkward. "You mean you remember the rest?"

George hesitated.

"Aww, c'mon, George!" needled Arish. "Think of it as . . . an educational exercise."

George gave him a flat look.

"Please?" Arish clasped his hands and widened his eyes.

"Jeez Louise," muttered George. "Go get the tables over there, if you feel like it." He took a deep breath. "I think the more times you sleep in the Glade, the more intense the dreams get. So when you wake up, there might be . . . afterimages."

Yikes. I didn't *want* to see more giant spiders. Yeah, it was fun when we were running around eating dream berries, but even though we beat them, the spiders were scary. I really thought we were going to die.

"So what you're saying," began Arish, not helping Eddy clean the other tables, "is that if we go back to the

Glade, we'll keep having cool dreams we remember in the morning?"

"You bet—wait, no! Don't do that!"

"You clearly tried it," said Eddy. "Doesn't that mean it's fine?"

"Oh fer Pete's sake, *no*!" *Tap-tap-taptaptap* came George's foot again. "I'm an Eagle Scout! I trained for this kind of stuff. But you're just kids, and someone already went missing. Dontcha know, it's not safe!"

Saliva flooded my mouth. My palms grew damp. I knew the others were already making plans to go back.

"You can't travel too far into the Glade either," George added. "When I walked around, I'd hear voices." I stiffened. Voices like the one I'd been hearing? "I don't know how big the inner world is, but something might live beyond its borders. Don't go far. Don't go, period!"

If something lived in the Glade, could it hurt us? Where did it come from? What would happen if we got stuck there, or lost? A gravity blanket felt strapped to my chest.

"You betcha," said Arish in an accent like George's.

"You're not listening." George wrung his hands. "I'm sorry I flew off the handle like that, but the Glade does something to you. I'd get so tired the more I slept there. The last time, I almost couldn't move when I woke up! I—"

"See, I told you they'd be in here," said a smug voice from the door. Bethany marched in, and Ms. Angela followed.

Eddy straightened. Arish dropped the rag, placing his hands behind his back. My knuckles grew white around the plate I gripped. Had they overheard us?

Ms. Angela caught the door before it closed. "Thank you, Bethany. Well, you four, as much as I'm sure George would be happy to talk to you, he has responsibilities." Ms. Angela didn't sound upset, but she was using a Teacher Voice (paired with Mom Look #1, *I Will Not Argue with You About This*). "Let's go back to where you're supposed to be, hmm? It's almost time to make bagged ice cream. I've never met anyone who didn't love ice cream."

Bethany stood behind her, looking pleased with herself.

George opened his mouth but closed it. Nothing he'd said had convinced the others not to go back . . . but would it be that bad if we did? If I could practice being Pina 2.0 in the Glade, it might be easier to do it in real

THE GLADE

life. Maybe next time, I could transform like the others and help save the day if a nightmare came to life. There had to be a safe way to explore the Glade's mysteries.

No surprise that I was getting in my head about it.

As we left, I didn't like the way Ms. Angela watched us, like she knew exactly what we'd been talking about.

NINE

Three nights later I was half asleep when the tapping came on the window next to my face. I jerked up so hard, I hit my head on the bottom of Jo's bunk. Ow! I rubbed the spot.

The knocking didn't stop.

I scrubbed the fog from the window. From behind a flashlight glow, two familiar faces grinned at me.

Over ice cream, after we talked to George the other day, Eddy and Arish said they wanted to go back to the Glade. Jo had agreed immediately, without asking what I thought, but suggested waiting until Eddy and I healed, which would get George off our tails and give us time to "prepare."

THE GLADE

Preparation meant spending arts and crafts making and painting papier-mâché heads. I grabbed mine from under my bed. Inside a hood and tucked under the covers, it could pass as me sleeping.

The sheets above my bunk rustled, and Jo climbed down the ladder. "Ready?" she whispered, already wearing her hoodie and sweatpants and carrying a pillow under her arm.

I filled the hoodie left in my bed with clothes and pulled a blanket over the fake me before grabbing my own pillow. I wasn't actually ready—I kept flashing through George's warnings—but I had to try.

Arish bounced on his toes when we joined them. "Are you psyched or what?" His voice was pretty loud for a whisper. "This is gonna be so cool!"

Eddy balanced his pillow on top of his head, clutching his action figure of Bombshell. "I bet we can control the dream better tonight since we know what we're in for." He smiled at Jo. "Right?"

Jo beamed. "Yup!"

Once again no one asked for my opinion. You know, the person whose nightmares had come to life last time? The person who had to save us from getting caught? What if this time, someone else's nightmares became real?

But despite myself, I was excited. George might have been in danger because he'd been alone; we weren't. My stomach clenched in what was definitely anticipation, not anxiety.

I rubbed my sweaty palms on my pants.

The woods were darker than they'd been the other nights. The boys shined flashlights so we could avoid tree roots and low-hanging branches. Eddy kept murmuring to Jo, which made me feel sick.

Did Jo notice I was hanging behind?

Did Jo even care?

Of course she did. The four of us were in this together. Eddy had been the one to flee the school-bus-sized spider with me; there was no reason to feel jealous.

Jo stepped back to help me over a particularly gnarly root, but I didn't let go of her hand. "Hey," I said. "We had fun last time, but it *was* scary. What if someone gets hurt tonight?"

To my shock, Jo shrugged and dropped my hand. "Don't chicken out now, P. Relax! It's gonna be fun." She turned to catch up with the others, leaving me behind.

Tears filled my eyes as my nose clogged. She hadn't

even bothered to check in with our code words. Sure, Jo always encouraged me to be brave, but she'd never . . . brushed me off like that before. Like I was annoying.

Like Eddy was more important to her.

I rubbed my eyes and hurried to catch up. I needed to quit being such a whiner. This was the summer of Pina 2.0, the new and improved version. Maybe Jo also wanted to become Jo 2.0. But what if Jo 2.0 didn't want me around?

Stop it, Pina! Eddy and Arish were important to me, too. That didn't mean Jo no longer mattered. And it didn't mean I no longer mattered to her, either. But it was one thing to tell myself that and another to fully believe it.

The walk wasn't long enough for me to stew. Unlike last time we didn't hear music to guide us; the clearing had stopped hiding once we'd found it. (It was a silly thought, but it felt that way.) Before long, we approached the ring of mushrooms. The perfume wasn't as heavy this time, but it did help me relax as I breathed it in.

"This is it!" Arish threw his pillow on the grass, swinging his arms one way and the next. "We ready to do this?"

"It'll be great." Eddy sounded a little nervous, like his

old worries had returned. I sort of hoped that was true. I didn't want to be the only one concerned.

"It *will* be great." Jo lay down and motioned for me to join her. More evidence she could have new friends and still care about me, since my annoying brain kept doubting that. "Remember, we'll be dreaming. We can control it. Right?"

"Right." Eddy sounded firmer. "Arish?"

"Totally." Arish placed his hands under his chin, elbows spread on his pillow. "Pina?"

I swallowed past the lump in my throat. "Yeah."

"You don't need to be afraid." Arish must have thought he was being encouraging because he smiled at me. "We're right here with you. And if we run into Ms. Angela again later, we know we can sneak past her. We already did it once."

"That's right." Jo placed her hand on my knee and squeezed. "We'll be together the whole time. Besides, don't you want to figure out how this place works, Dr. Scientist?"

That got me to smile.

"And"—Eddy waved Bombshell—"we can protect each other again."

THE GLADE

That was true. We'd fought an army and won because we'd been together. Even I'd contributed from my hiding spot.

I could be brave with my friends.

I settled into my makeshift bed, holding Jo's hand. This time when I looked up at the stars, I tried to be excited. My friends were with me. I hadn't heard—

Welcome back, Pina. . . .

The musty smell of damp dirt woke me. I was back in that dark room, feeling like a caterpillar in a cocoon. Unlike the confusion of last time, I was prepared.

This was the Glade.

My fingers found the knob right away, and I pushed the door open and stumbled out, almost tripping on a giant root. Steadying myself, I turned to look at the room I'd arrived in. While the inside was too dark to see details, the outside was like a giant tree trunk. As I looked up and up, there were no branches or a treetop I could see. The brown towers shot into the clouds, and when I ran my fingers over the trunk, I didn't feel bark but a soft, spongy texture.

"Hellooooooo, Pina!"

I turned. Arish bounded toward me. "We made it back! Welcome to La Gladé!"

Uh, why had he said it like that? Was he trying to be funny?

"Did you get a look at the door?" He swung the door to my not-trunk closed. "Whoa! It's different from mine!"

My door was grass green, and delicate sketches of my favorite plants covered it: mouth-headed snapdragons (*Antirrhinum* species), coned *Echinacea*, the red leaves of a Japanese maple (*Acer palmatum*). I traced the bumps and grooves of the images, dry but not brittle to my touch. Under a weeping willow (*Salix babylonica*) were a pile of books and a hero's sword balanced atop them. The book spines didn't have names, but they were colored black, white, green, and gray.

Arish's door was midnight blue plastered with gold stars and a spaceship flying across it. A floppy chair had MR. DIRECTOR written on the back in magenta, yellow, and blue; a megaphone swung from an arm. A laptop, some gadgets, and Arish's signature glasses were painted on the door too.

"It's so cool, right?" he said. "It's like this place knows us!"

THE GLADE

Which was . . . a little eerie.

A crash sounded behind us. We spun to see Jo stumbling out of another trunk and Eddy cautiously peering out of his. Their doors were also decorated specifically for them—Eddy's had *Unicorn Quest* characters in Bombshell's colors of pink, blue, and purple; and Jo's was a yellow, white, purple, and black tapestry of her favorite *DynoHunters* characters.

"It's as amazing as I remembered," said Eddy. "We're really dreaming the same dream? You're not people I made up?"

"I'm me," said Arish. "You think you could dream up this magnificence?"

Eddy snorted. "Yeah, right. Forget I asked."

"Kaya mo ba, P?" Jo checked me over for any scrapes.

"Khoobam." I smiled as my belly somersaulted from her concern.

We'd done it. We were dreaming in the clearing and had made it to the Glade.

The last dream had started out fun before it got scary. Would this dream be the same, or would it be worse, like spiders tumbling from the sky? Or something else one of us feared?

Jo looked back at her trunk-portal-thing before looking up, as I had. "Did we come down from there?" she asked. "Is that the clearing?"

The question distracted me enough to break me out of my gloom and doom. "Huh! I think you're right." I didn't know how or why, but I was certain I was no longer *above*. My friends and I were *below*. Not underground, perhaps, but under *some*thing. The sky overhead looked like the sky I knew at first glance, but the more I stared at it, the more it looked a bit too gray, a bit too brown. And a lot like gills.

Mushrooms?

"What are we waiting for?" demanded Arish. "It's adventure time!" And like before, Arish transformed into a super space spy, a cape flaring out from his space suit, his secret agent glasses flicking on.

"What if I want to be a supersecret spy too?" Jo grinned, whirling in the lichen-moss as a cape of her own enveloped her. When she stopped, hopping on one foot as she regained balance, she was wearing a sparkly purple suit and a silver top hat, the cape gone. A robot dog barked, running around her. "Ta-da! And my robotic companion!"

THE GLADE

"Ooh, ooh, I know! You're the Doctor from *Doctor When*!" Eddy bounced on his toes, glowing in his magical girl transformation. Instead of metal, his armor this time was leather, and he held his staff aloft. "C'mon, Pina, your turn!"

If thinking about my nightmares brought them to life, I'd rather think about dreams. I hadn't gotten a chance to change before, but without fear clouding my brain, I could focus. Who did I want to become tonight? I tapped my chin, then smiled. "Got it. I bet I can race you to the top of the hill and be transformed before you can see!"

The others dashed. I imagined I could feel a jetpack settling onto my shoulders and strapping to my thighs as I leapt into the air. I couldn't picture it, but I could tell myself it had happened. Tonight I was going to be Jamie Einstein, Girl Genius, ready to solve any problem with science at her side.

It was time to put our imaginations to the test. And no spiders or singing kids would stop us.

How far could we control the Glade? Arish concentrated until he created a tea party, complete with a Mad Hatter statue, and Eddy danced around the table as flowers sprang in his wake before kicking into a cartwheel.

I harvested flowers made of cookie wafers, and Eddy, twirling his staff, yelled, "Let there be cake!" A burst of confetti revealed a platter with a three-tiered chocolate dessert.

"This is the coolest place ever!" Arish threw his head back and cackled.

We enjoyed our party. The frosting melted on my tongue, a perfect match for the hot tea. But Jo kept tapping her feet and jiggling her legs. "Let's explore!" she said. "Want to see who can find the most different kinds of berries?" She pointed to a patch of bushes we could see from the top of the hill. "Time starts now!"

Activating my jetpack, I watched the capes stream behind my friends. Jo transformed her robot dog into a scooter and clung to her hat as she kicked. I grinned, gliding into loop the loops, happy to let them win.

How could I have been afraid of this place? The Glade could make our wildest dreams come true. We were too powerful here to let any silly spiders stop us. Anything we wanted could happen as long as we imagined it.

(Okay, spiders weren't silly, but still!)

I rotated to admire the landscape. The same mushroom-trees dotted the horizon, but there was also a mushroom forest closer by. Behind our party leftovers

THE GLADE

were our trunks—our stem-trunks?—where we'd come into the Glade. Ahead of me were the bushes where my friends hunched, looking for berries.

And there was a fifth stem-trunk twisting into the not-sky.

Curious, I zoomed over, lowering myself until I could touch down in front of it.

Unlike the stem-trunks we'd used, this one was ancient. It looked like a gnarled, leafless tree, curving around itself, and I couldn't tell if it was topped with domes or gills like a real mushroom. Our doors had been personalized to us, but the art on this one was too faded to make out. Instead, vines wrapped and sealed the entrance.

I stepped closer and brushed off the layer of dirt on the door. Grooves met my fingers, and if I squinted, I could make out a few shapes. Concentrating, I let my fingertips explore, making out the letters *D* and *S*.

The vines rippled like snakes, tightening around the stem-trunk. Orange and purple leaves with five tips splayed out like hands. If they'd been green and thinner stemmed, they'd have looked a lot like Virginia creepers. (Unless the vines "above" weren't actually Virginia creepers?) I reached to stroke the fuzzy flesh of the fingers-thick stem.

Ring around the mushroom . . .

"Ouch!" Sucking on my finger where I'd pricked it, I looked around for the voice. Something rustled, but the only things nearby were the vines trailing on the ground. Their thorns gleamed, and the one that had pricked me was as big as my pinky. But it hadn't been there a moment ago. . . .

The stem-trunk was covered in more than vines. Mushrooms peppered its surface—how had I missed them?—some as tiny as my thumbnail and some as large as my palm. One cluster of skinny mushrooms was as orange as the lichen-moss; another group was squat and electric blue, with a lone purple puffball growing nearby, and nowhere did I see a species I knew. I examined one growing where a doorknob would be. The green-yellow cap looked familiar. Lavender powder puffed into my face, and I sneezed. Rosewater? Perfume?

Long enough to build your tomb . . .

I tried to block out the voice to think. Unlike with our doors, the marks were too faded on this one to give any indication of who it could belong to. The letters I'd felt told me nothing. Could there be someone else asleep above? Or, since the stem-trunk looked so old, did it no longer work?

THE GLADE

There was so much about the Glade we didn't understand. Our imaginations controlled this place, but *how*? Where had it come from? If someone else came down here, would the Glade listen to them or to us? My breath quickened. What the heck was I thinking, playing down here as if there would be no consequences when I woke up?

I needed to wake up.

Forget her...

Forget her...

Forget her? Who did the voice want me to forget? The back of my neck prickled. The last time I'd felt like this, an army of spiders had rolled into view. Spiders and I would never like each other, but I was prepared this time. I could defeat them as long as I was with my friends.

Speaking of...

You're too late!

The voice giggled. If I'd been awake, I might have puked.

"Jo?" came Eddy's voice. "Jo, hey, where are you going?"

I whipped around. The mushroom forest had sprung up around me and blocked my view. My arm slid against a thorn, a long scratch blooming on my skin. I hissed, slapping a hand over the cut. The vines around me coiled closer. They were twice the size they'd been a moment ago.

I couldn't breathe. I needed to move, but my limbs didn't listen to my commands. My legs quivered.

"Jo, come back!" said Arish. "We don't know what's over there! Jo!"

I needed to get to the others, and fast. I tried to fire up my jetpack, but I was shaking too hard to use it. The vines rustled, loosely circling one of my legs, then the other. If I tried to remove my foot, I'd prick myself on those giant thorns.

My mouth was so dry. But if I didn't get myself out of this, I'd be too late to help Jo.

Turning my spine to steel, I shut my eyes, thinking about the sword from my stem-trunk door. A heavy weight slid into my hand. I hacked at the plants with the blade until they recoiled, snaking back toward the rotting stem-trunk.

I felt a bit guilty harming plant life, but my friends were in trouble.

Freed, I leapt over another vine worming its way toward me and ran through the mushroom forest. The forest was too packed to use my jetpack, so it disappeared off my back. The ground squelched underneath my feet, sinking with each step like quicksand, but I pushed through.

Jo needed me. I had to be brave for her. And despite the familiar fear choking me, I had to prove to myself that I could be brave for my friends in any tough situation.

It took eight hundred hours, but I finally crashed out of the mushroom forest, falling to my knees. Trying to catch my breath, I looked up to see Eddy and Arish standing at a riverbank. I hadn't seen this river when I'd been flying about. Where had it come from? Was it the same river Eddy had mentioned last time?

"Pina!" Arish helped me up. "You gotta do something!"

"What happened?" I brushed off the dirt from my knees. Eddy stood at the foot of a rickety wooden bridge, but he wouldn't step forward—or couldn't. The area closer to the bridge felt heavy, like pushing through honey.

"Jo wandered off while we were berry picking," he said. "We thought they'd found more bushes, but then—"

"Then we found them here," continued Arish. "I think she made the bridge herself, like how we do our outfits?" He pushed his secret agent glasses up to rub his face. "It was like she was hypnotized. We've been calling to them for ages, but she won't come back."

"Why didn't you follow her?" I asked, but my own feet felt glued to the ground. George's warning about not wandering far rang in my ears. Plus, while I didn't see any barrier, I could *feel* one. And that bridge did not look safe.

"I'm scared," said Eddy. "What's happening to them?"

"Jo!" hollered Arish. "Jo, c'mon, we gotta go!"

Across the river, wide and deep as it rushed past, Jo stood with her back to us. She didn't look over as we called her name. Instead, she stepped forward.

I managed to lift one foot and place it closer to the bridge, but I hit something that definitely wasn't ground.

The cap Jo always wore, the one I'd given her, was caked with mud beneath my foot.

The memory of what the little kid's voice had sung minutes ago echoed in my head: *Forget her, forget her, you're too late!* I pinched myself. That creepy, fake nursery rhyme wasn't about Jo—it couldn't be. She was right there.

But her cap . . . She loved this cap because *I'd* given it to her. What did it mean that it was abandoned? Did that say something about our friendship?

THE GLADE

"Jo!" I shouted, my voice cracking. "George told us not to wander! You gotta come back!"

She hesitated.

"Come back to us!" cried Eddy.

"C'mon, Jo!" called Arish.

Why she'd left the cap was meaningless. It had to be. This was a dream—a nightmare.

"Jo, please," I pleaded. "I need you."

That finally made her turn around. She took a few steps toward us as Arish cheered her on, but she kept glancing over her shoulder. When her feet hit the planks of her bridge, I was able to breathe. When she crossed back over, I threw my arms around her. Arish and Eddy joined our hug. Jo didn't like people touching her, but she seemed okay with the boys.

When we drew back, I asked, "Khoobee?"

"I thought I heard my name," she mumbled, rubbing her forehead. "I could have sworn . . ."

She looked back over the river. Her bridge was gone.

"You mean the little kid?" Thank goodness someone else had heard them again!

Jo shook her head. "What kid?"

Just kidding.

"The one singing nursery rhymes . . . ?" I trailed off

when I saw the looks on my friends' faces. If this was bad, then I definitely didn't want to tell them that sometimes I thought I heard the same voice topside.

"Wait, we heard something last time, didn't we?" asked Eddy. "'The Itsy-Bitsy Spider,' right? The Glade has a bad sense of humor."

"I haven't heard it since, though," said Arish.

I forced a laugh. The last thing I wanted was for my new friends to stop talking to me over this. "Yeah, maybe! Anyway, not sure about you, but I think I'm done for tonight." I knelt to retrieve Jo's cap, but it was gone. I tried not to dwell on what that could mean either.

"Let's get out of here," agreed Eddy. "I've had enough of this place."

Annoyance flashed through me—I'd been saying this whole time that the Glade was dangerous!—but it was gone as soon as it came. I'd been having fun earlier too. I'd pushed back my usual worries again and again. Maybe I shouldn't have. My usual worries kept us safe.

"How do we wake up?" I tried not to sound as nervous as I felt, taking Jo's hand.

"Don't you remember?" said Eddy. "We go back in those tree trunks."

"Tree-tubes," corrected Arish.

"I've been calling them stem-trunks." I was glad it was a simple solution. "I don't think they're trees."

Jo said nothing. I hoped she'd feel better when we woke up.

We headed back to our trunks. I opened the door to Jo's. She stared at the darkness for a long moment before shaking her head and stepping inside. What had happened to her across the river? If it hadn't been the weird kid, whose voice had she heard? And for that matter, what was with the voice I kept hearing that the others didn't? Disturbed, I closed her door and headed back to my own trunk.

It was easier than I expected to wake up. One moment I was closing my door; the next I was opening my eyes, hearing birds twittering in the background. Like that, I was back. Beside me Jo stirred, and I heard Arish yawn.

"Well, well, well."

My stomach dropped.

"You four are in so much trouble," said Mean Girl Bethany, grinning down at us.

TEN

"See, I told you!" Bethany crowed to George. "I *knew* they were breaking the rules!"

George shook his head as he told us to gather our pillows and follow them out of the forest. The sun was much, much higher than it should have been, which meant we'd overslept.

I should have stayed up.

The trudge through the woods felt twice as long as before. Arish kept stumbling into Eddy, Eddy kept yawning, and Jo walked like a zombie. "Exhausted" didn't begin to cover how I felt as my limbs swam through honey. More like achy, dead on my feet, and a little nauseous.

THE GLADE

George stayed silent as he led us to Ms. Angela's cabin, where he opened the door for us. On the path outside, leading to the entryway, sprawled Virginia creepers—or were they actually the vines from the Glade?

The cabin looked the same as the last time Eddy and I had been in it. George and Bethany led us to a room at the back. George knocked, though the door was open. "We found them!" chirped Bethany, shoving us inside.

Ms. Angela sat at a big wooden desk. She turned in her chair, mouth pursed: Mom Look #15, *I Expected Better from You*. We must have looked silly standing in front of her with our pillows, none of us meeting her gaze.

There was a window overlooking her garden, and a door, propped open, that led directly outside. My fingers itched to take care of whatever she'd planted, but I was already in enough trouble.

Maybe one day I could earn my freedom back from my parents. Time for three million lectures and two hundred years of grounding. So long, Pina 2.0!

"I'm very disappointed in the four of you." Ms. Angela now sported Mom Look #3, *Time for a Serious Discussion*. "We trust you to be your best selves at Camp Clear Skies. These weeks are meant for you to learn and grow and make lifelong connections, and the rules are there to facilitate that—and to keep you safe. The middle of the night, and no one knew where you were! What if someone had gotten hurt? What if you'd gotten lost? What could have possibly compelled you to sneak off like that?"

George shifted from one foot to the other. Arish opened his mouth, then closed it. Eddy stared at his feet. Jo looked dazed, as if she hadn't fully woken up, her pillow dragging on the floor.

We couldn't tell Ms. Angela about the Glade. We couldn't tell *anyone*.

The cut on my forearm itched. I scratched it absently, then focused. I'd gotten cut in my dream. . . .

My mind whirled, putting together my observations.

At last, Ms. Angela sighed. "I hope this little lesson will stick. Consider this your first and final warning. One more incident and I'll be calling your guardians to pick you up. Is that understood?"

Warning? We weren't getting kicked out? I was so relieved, I could have collapsed on the ground and kissed her feet. I clutched my pillow to my chest and nodded with the others.

"Now, if you don't mind, I'd like a word with George.

THE GLADE

Please wait outside. We clearly cannot trust you to go back to camp activities on your own."

That was embarrassing. I was the first one out and the one to close the door behind us.

"I hope you learned your lesson," said Bethany. "Why were you in the forest, anyway? Dorky loser stuff?"

"Why'd you rat us out?" demanded Eddy. "We never did anything to you."

"Causing trouble *is* doing stuff to me!" She twirled her ponytail. "I can't wait to tell Molly. She's definitely going to let me be an assistant counselor. She thought I was making things up, but nope, I caught you red-handed!"

"Whatever," muttered Eddy.

"Quiet!" snapped Arish, his ear pressed to the door. "I'm trying to listen!"

Eddy stomped a foot. "Haven't we gotten in enough trouble already?"

"Yeah," sneered Bethany, but she stepped over to eavesdrop too.

Arish flapped a hand, making room for Bethany. To me, Eddy said, "So much for our adventures. How do you think the Glade works, anyway? It's like magic!"

"Do you know about the bacteria in our bodies?"

I asked. He shook his head. This was one medical fact I did find cool. "They're everywhere, covering our skin and in our mouths and stuff, and a gazillion live in our guts to help us digest food. Plants and funguses—fungi," I corrected, remembering one of Mom's lectures on terminology. It felt like a hundred years ago. "Fungi act for plants like bacteria do for us. Remember how I told you about the mycelium network?" That also felt like a hundred years ago. "With the mushrooms down there, I bet we tapped into an underground root system, which let us dream but also kept us connected to our bodies."

"Wow," breathed Eddy. "That's cool."

"And dangerous. Look." Tucking my pillow against my chest with my elbows, I pushed up my sleeve to show the scratch on my arm from the vine. Eddy reached to touch it, then drew back. "This happened in the dream. Whatever happens in the Glade can affect us up here. Ms. Angela was right. We could have gotten hurt with no one to help us."

Eddy's mouth flattened into a line, and he nodded. "Maybe that's why I'm so tired and sore. I feel like I was up doing cartwheels. I guess I sort of was."

THE GLADE

Arish, with another wave, shushed us again, and Ms. Angela's voice came through the door.

". . . so guard them until midnight. They don't need to know you won't be there all night. Make sure to tell Molly. I know you couldn't have predicted this, but I'm disappointed. You know those kids. Your twelve-year-old sister shouldn't be more reliable than my head counselor."

Bethany preened. Eddy and I rolled our eyes at each other.

"Do you have anything to say for yourself, George?"

"Nope," said George's voice, sounding closer than Ms. Angela's.

Arish sprang back, dragging Bethany with him, a moment before the office door opened. George stepped out, not looking at us. Ms. Angela stood in the doorway, hands on her hips, watching us head back to camp.

The entire time, Jo said absolutely nothing.

The whole day Jo was quiet and moody. When we joined the others from our group—after Bethany had gleefully lectured us on behaving ourselves and said that she'd be watching past midnight—Kiki, Mackenzie, and Constance wanted to know where we'd been. I gave them a half-truth: we'd wanted to see what it was like to sleep in the woods and had gotten caught. "I could have told you what it's like," said Mackenzie, whose family liked camping. "Sheesh!"

That night, as everyone prepared for bed, Jo swung down from her bunk and sat beside me. I shifted to give her room and put my book down.

For a long time she didn't say anything while picking at a loose thread on my sheets. I leaned against the wall. Jo didn't like talking about what upset her, so she needed a little prodding before opening up.

"What are you thinking about?" I kept my voice low.

She sighed and dropped her head in her hands. "My mom."

That wasn't the answer I expected. "What about her?"

Jo kept her face in her hands for a while before sitting back. "I used to call her every week." She traced the creases of the underside of her mattress. "Sometimes she'd be excited to talk and would spend the whole time rambling about stuff, but a lot of times she was too tired to say much. Or she wouldn't bother to come to the phone. She's not allowed her own, so I'd have to wait until patient call hours. Aunt Lyd said the doctors told her I was upsetting Mom and to stop calling so much. So I started calling once a month instead, and things seemed okay. But . . ." She dropped her hand and shut her eyes. "The last time we talked was six months ago. They must have changed her meds again, because she yelled at me and told me to stop bothering her. I haven't called since, and neither has she."

I put my hand on hers. I could only imagine how much that hurt.

She exhaled, her fingers closing around mine. "I can't remember what happened across the river. I didn't realize there was a river until I was on the other side. One moment I was picking berries, and the next I heard someone calling for me. I . . . thought it was her."

Oh. No wonder she'd been weird today.

"I know it's ridiculous," she added. "It doesn't make sense. But it *felt* real."

I nodded. Everything in the Glade felt more real than our world. When anything was possible below, why couldn't Jo's mom also be around?

It was scary how much the Glade knew about us. From our doors to Jo's mom, it was like it could read our minds. What if, instead of us controlling the Glade, the Glade could control *us*? What if every time we went down there, the Glade got to know us more and more? If that voice that I'd been hearing was a part of the Glade, it already knew my name. Too many stories and myths talked about the power of names for me not to be concerned.

My stomach lurched, dinner sloshing around.

Jo didn't notice my shudder. "Aunt Lyd and Uncle Brock don't want me around. My mom doesn't want me. My dad's family didn't want me. I feel like . . ." She rubbed her face. "I don't know. I don't look like Aunt Lyd or like Mom, but I don't know the first thing about being Filipino either."

That much I already knew. Last year Jo had been the one to come up with our code words. She'd found a book in the school library that taught her a few words in Tagalog, and that's how I decided to ask my dad about the words in Persian. She'd hidden that book from her aunt and uncle; why hadn't I asked *why*?

"I've never even had Filipino food before," she said. "Aunt Lyd says it smells funny, but I wouldn't know. A lot of times I think my aunt and uncle don't want me to be Filipino. They tell me it's too bad my mom didn't get with 'a nice American boy.' But I don't get it—my dad's in my mom's high school yearbook. Or, at least, someone I think is him. I tried to convince Aunt Lyd that if they found my dad's family, then I could live with them instead. She laughed! She said no one would want me. Uncle Brock says my dad's family lives in huts without running water, and I should be grateful we live in America."

My shoulders stiffened. I'd known Aunt Lyd and Uncle Brock were mean, but I didn't appreciate how mean. Why would they think Jo's Filipino family wouldn't love her? Why would they make her feel so bad about being who she was?

"Then there's everything else," continued Jo. "I don't think I'm a girl, but I'm not a boy. I'm not smart like you. I don't have a 'thing' that I'm good at or know what I want to be when I grow up. I feel . . . I guess I feel like an alien walking around humans. I've never belonged anywhere, you know?"

My ears rang. Was she saying what I thought she was? How could Jo think she didn't fit in *anywhere* because her aunt and uncle were jerks? Brave, fierce Jo. Jo, my protector. Jo, my best friend in the whole world.

"But when we were down there," she said, "the Glade . . . *chose* me. It's, like, I finally found a place that wants me around. A place where I belong."

My heard pounded. "You do belong, though. You'll always have a place with me."

"But I'm not going to be around to protect you forever," she snapped out of nowhere, ripping her hand away. "Not once the summer ends and we move!"

I clutched my palm to my chest, trying not to shrink from her. "You're . . . moving?"

Jo's annoyance vanished. Her shoulders sagged. "Uncle Brock got a job in Detroit for a lot of money. He's supposed to start in September. His company found us a place to stay. I haven't known how to tell you. I've been trying to for a while. But you . . . I knew you'd be upset."

My breathing was too loud. The things she hadn't been saying for weeks clicked into place.

"You were so excited about camp. I didn't want to spoil it. I figured there'd be time after. But . . ."

I couldn't look at her. If I did, I'd have to think about her leaving, and if I thought about her leaving, I'd get upset, and if I got upset, I'd make Jo feel bad. I didn't want to make her feel worse. It wasn't like she asked Uncle Brock to find a new job.

"Sorry for snapping at you."

I blinked back tears. "It's okay."

THE GLADE

After a few tense moments Jo mumbled a good night and climbed into her bed. A couple minutes later Counselor Molly ordered lights-out.

I stared at the bottom of Jo's bunk. Maybe if I stared hard enough, everything around me would crack, and I'd break into a million pieces. With no way to put me back together again, I'd be swept into the garbage with the crumbs and dust bunnies.

Jo moving? Jo not coming over every day after school, every weekend? Not being in my classes, defending me against bullies, doing homework with me, going to the library together, keeping me company in the garden, having dinner with my parents?

How could I possibly be Pina 2.0 without Jo beside me?

I stuffed my pillow into my mouth, hoping no one—especially Jo—could hear me cry. Snot smeared against the fabric as I tried to muffle my hiccups. Tears soaked my pillowcase.

Eventually, I must have fallen asleep, because I woke with a pounding headache. I groaned, light shining onto my face. The room was dark, but from the window pulsed a familiar yellow-green glow.

The Glade.

The air felt stuffy, like a fouler camp smell. Half expecting to hear the creepy kid, I slid from my bed and stepped onto the ladder. "Jo?"

Her bed was empty.

My heart thudded like a drum, louder than when Jo had snapped at me. I dropped back to the floor, shoved my feet into my shoes, and grabbed a hoodie.

Then I remembered Ms. Angela's warning and Molly's guard and Bethany's nosiness. I tiptoed through the silent cabin, holding my breath whenever I passed by a bunk. If I got caught, I'd be kicked out, no questions asked.

But if Molly or Bethany had been awake, Jo would still be in bed.

No one was outside, as I'd suspected. After easing the screen door open and shut, I took a deep breath, squared my shoulders, and went to find the above-world entrance to the Glade.

The glow through the trees guided my way until I stood outside the ring of mushrooms. They pulsed, sending the perfume spores my way. I yawned, then slapped my cheek. This was no time for dreams.

Inside the clearing lay a sleeping Jo. If we headed back right away, we should be able to avoid the counselors and getting in trouble. Keeping my ears peeled for any noises, I knelt and shook Jo's shoulder.

She didn't stir.

I shook harder, but that didn't wake her either. I yelled her name right in her ear, but again, nothing. Finally, I grabbed both shoulders and hauled her up.

She opened her eyes. It worked!

Except it hadn't, because her eyes rolled to the top of her head to reveal the whites, like I was in a horror movie.

How many times had I thought that this week?

This could only mean one thing: Jo was in trouble, and I was the only one who could help.

ELEVEN

I didn't hesitate. Easing Jo down, I lay next to her and closed my eyes.

Sleep came quickly. I was back in my stem-trunk before I knew it, but when I pushed the door, it wouldn't budge.

My throat tightened. If I didn't get out of here, who knew where Jo could end up—and what could end up with her.

There was no room to turn around, and the space was dark and dank. If I'd been lying down, I'd have been convinced I'd been buried alive.

My lungs couldn't get enough air. My palms were

going to sweat until my skin peeled off, and then they'd get infected, and a gazillion bacteria would eat through my hands and travel into my bloodstream to devour the rest of me from the inside out.

I couldn't breathe I couldn't breathe I couldn't—

Digging my nails into my palms, I forced myself to calm down by counting to one hundred. Deep breaths brought the smell of compost and made me hiccup, so instead, I focused on the grooves my sharp nails left in my soft skin. I couldn't freak out, not when Jo needed me. No one knew we were down here, not even Eddy and Arish.

I tried pushing on the handle again, and it gave a little. It wasn't a real door, so it wasn't locked!

I shoved against it, and it gave a little more, light slipping through the crack. Right. Okay. I maneuvered in the tight space and pressed my shoulder against the door. One, two . . .

On three, I shoved hard enough to get a hand, then an arm, then an elbow through, and I squirmed my way out. Collapsing on the mossy ground, I turned to see heavy rocks at the base of my door.

Why wouldn't Jo want me to follow her? Since she was

moving, were we no longer friends? Did she not want me around anymore?

No! I couldn't start thinking like that. Something was wrong—Jo wasn't acting like herself. Best friends stuck together. If I were acting weird, I'd want her to snap me out of it.

Determined, I pushed myself up. I shut my eyes and imagined my jetpack sliding onto my shoulders and my sword at my waist. As usual I couldn't picture it for real, but I'd gotten the hang of the Glade's powers last time. When I felt the comforting weights at my back and hip, I made sure my items were secured and launched into the sky.

I surveyed the land until I found the river. There was no way to ignore the funk—too sweet, three steps past ripe—wafting from that direction. A figure stood on the other side; it had to be Jo. I tilted the jetpack that way.

But the closer I flew, the heavier I felt, like the environment was changing to stop me. A force pressed me down and down and down until I had to land.

While I could stand, the atmosphere still felt unpleasant, coating me like a sticky layer of sunscreen. If I stared into space, the air began to shimmer and twist together, changing shapes—first a spider, then a human, then a bulbous shadow atop eight twisted legs.

Batting my hand to dispel the images, I jogged (as much as I could) in the direction I'd seen Jo. The air had thickened, turning smoky gray. That post-ripeness odor strengthened. My skin felt greasy.

Finally, I saw Jo on the other side of the river. I called her name, but she didn't move, as if she didn't—or couldn't—hear me. The fog swept over me, filling my nose and mouth with an earthy taste.

Hush, little baby, don't be absurd.
None of your wishes will ever be heard.

I inhaled a sharp fragrance. The scent was familiar. And so was that high-pitched singing. Didn't I know that voice? Hadn't I heard it before?

I shook my head, as if it would loosen the cobwebs in my mind. I needed to focus. I needed to . . . Why was I here again? Where were the others?

The others—right. Jo. I was here for Jo. Both my body and mind were moving through molasses.

"Jo!" I called again, coughing. "Jo, I'm here! Come back over!"

She didn't move.

I gritted my teeth. The river between us grew deeper, the water roaring past. It was so loud, I could barely hear my own shouts.

The fog blanketed our surroundings. Jo became a silhouette. If I didn't do something fast, I'd lose sight of her.

And if your hopes and plans were all set,
I'll lull you to sleep until you forget.

I shut my eyes and thought about a big, safe fire. I wasn't sure if it would work, but soon, I felt the crackling heat. The light cast by the bonfire forced the fog to dome around us.

The lingering haze in my mind cleared. I knew what to do. I needed a way to cross—a big bridge, sturdy enough to support both me and Jo.

Bricks flew out of nowhere to arch over the water, building faster and faster until a red bridge with rails went from one bank to the other. I poked the bridge with my toe before placing my weight onto it. The light of the fire kept the fog at bay far enough that I could see the other side. I could make it.

And if bad nightmares bog down your dreams,
I'll stay awake to hear all your screams.

The voice was morphing with every verse. It had been

a little kid's at first, but with each line of the changed nursery rhyme, it sounded more and more wrong, like someone had run it through an auto-tune app. Could it be whomever—or whatever—Good Guy George thought lived within or beyond the Glade?

Two steps before the bridge ended, a patch of gray hung in the air where the light of the fire no longer reached. Readying my mind to go fuzzy for a few seconds, I pushed forward.

The moment I stepped out of the light, the fog devoured the world.

And if you scream your throat too hoarse,
I'll have no choice but to use brute force.

My ears filled the way they did underwater. My eyes were open, but I couldn't see anything. My body remembered being imprisoned in the stem-trunk and reacted: my breaths got shallower and shallower, and my stomach threatened to upchuck every meal I'd ever eaten, and my shoulders squeezed so hard, the pressure was sure to pop my eyeballs out of my skull.

Why wasn't the Glade helping me like it had before? Had I done something wrong? Did it have to do with the singing voice?

I needed to . . . move!

You'll have nothing that isn't from me.

Once you are mine, you'll never be free.

"Pina is such a good influence on her," came another voice I knew but couldn't place.

"Jo's a good girl," said an even more familiar voice. "Proserpina can't do anything without her."

"Oh, come on, Grace," said Voice #1. "Josephine would get into even more trouble without Pina to keep her on the straight and narrow. I swear she gets it from that no-good father of hers. My sister was never like this when we were kids."

"Now, Lyd," said Voice #2 with a nervous laugh. "You don't mean that."

"It's just us here, Grace; no need to be politically correct. Ray-za's one of the good ones, but Jose was—heck, what he wanted was an anchor baby to bring the rest of his freeloading family over. It's a good thing he died in Afghanistan before he could."

Fake or real, I'd heard enough. Those voices wanted to keep me from Jo, and I'd never let that happen. Gritting my teeth, I shoved forward until I tore through the mist and collapsed on the other side of the river.

When I looked behind me, the fog was gone. The

THE GLADE

heaviness remained on my skin, though, and in my heart.

So did the wrong lyrics of those nursery rhymes. That was the third one, and each had gotten worse.

And that conversation between Mom and Aunt Lyd had sounded real.

There wasn't time to get stuck. I pushed myself up. Jo stared out into the distance.

The back of my neck prickled. Someone was watching us. No—someone else was here with us! Could it be the owner of the voice? Who were they? The owner of the abandoned stem-trunk? The missing kid from the old camp?

This wasn't the time.

I ran up to Jo and shook her. Like she had in the world above, she didn't respond, continuing to stand around, glassy-eyed.

You're not supposed to be here, snapped the voice of the singing kid. *They're mine! You can't have her!*

"*You* can't have her!" I grabbed Jo's arm and tugged. She was rooted like a tree.

The voice laughed. *Oh yes, I can. They're strong, and you're weak. I don't want you. Who'd want scared little Pina? You're useless.*

I froze. The voice had changed again, but into one

I'd heard moments ago. It was the voice in my head that scolded me.

It was Mom.

You're not a hero, said Mom. *You're a whiny little girl who can't do anything without her best friend. Soon she'll leave you, and you'll be alone.*

My eyes stung. She was right. Jo would move with her family and forget about me. Jo, who was figuring out who she was without me. Jo, who might wake up one day and not remember my name.

Just Pina, afraid of spiders, crooned Mom. *Itsy-bitsy Pina, fly away home. Play by yourself and die in the loam.*

The threat jolted me.

Even when Mom was mad, she didn't *hate* me!

Die in the loam? No way!

(Loam was a soil mix that had lots of nutrients for plants but was sandy enough for water to drain rather than rot the roots. I'd read about loam in one of my library books and told Mom I wanted to make our own soil mix depending on each plant's needs. Mom had turned it into a research project, but I hadn't minded. Every time we talked about it, she'd give me Mom Look #6, *Pleased,* which didn't happen often.)

That's right. This couldn't be Mom, because Mom wasn't here. This was the Glade, or something within it, which sounded like my mom. How did it know?

Jo stepped forward. She reached out, but not to me—to the space in front of her. Her fingers curled, like someone had taken her hand.

I swiped at my eyes and grabbed Jo's free arm. Whatever was on her other side tugged. This presence that had pretended to be my mom, which had probably faked that conversation between Mom and Aunt Lyd, was trying to take Jo away.

I couldn't let them. I had to be brave and strong for Jo, like she was always brave and strong for me. For once I would be *her* protector.

This time, as I held Jo's arm, my feet dragging against the lichen-moss, I concentrated on the tingle I'd felt when I'd grown the lavender days ago. No one could stop me from saving Jo, even if it meant dragging her out of here myself.

I was strong and tough. And I'd save my best friend.

My jetpack settled on my shoulders, and my sword hung on my waist. Letting go of Jo for a second, I lunged in front of her, slashing with my sword. The force pulling her shrieked, but I didn't give it a chance to fight back. I grabbed Jo and turned on my jetpack, which stuttered for a heart-stopping moment. Before I could panic, I shoved the throttle down and adjusted my grip on Jo's wrist, hauling her across the bridge and away from the river. The jetpack managed to push through the invisible force.

The presence slithered after us.

Jo didn't dig in her heels, but she wasn't exactly helping either. Fortunately, as we moved farther from the bridge, the pressure lessened. The Glade couldn't have Jo, no matter what. I'd make sure of it.

We got to our stem-trunks. There were only two of them, mine and Jo's, but Jo's didn't look like it had before. The *DynoHunters* characters were there, but they were faded. And new colors had sprouted—in the form of those mysterious, unclassified mushrooms. Orange and purple and blue.

A thorny vine twisted at the base.

This was bad, but we didn't have time to deal with it. I opened the door and shoved Jo in, slamming it shut behind her. I waited until the trunk shimmered like the air on a hot day before running to my own and climbing inside.

THE GLADE

When I opened my eyes, I was back above, in the clearing. Jo breathed quietly, and when I sat up, her eyes opened. The sun was rising. My entire body ached.

Jo turned her head toward me, blinking. "P . . . ?"

"Are you okay?" I didn't bother with code words. I pressed the back of my hand to her forehead like my parents did when I was sick. She was warm but not fever hot. "What happened?"

"I . . ." She turned her head away from my hand. Her skin was ashen, her breathing shaky. "The river . . ." She coughed. "We should . . ." She trailed off, blinking slowly.

Something was definitely wrong. Something *felt* wrong. Jo was back with me, but she wasn't herself. Like a part of her was left behind in the Glade, and someone—or something—else had hitched along instead.

TWELVE

Over breakfast Jo was back to her usual self, although I felt tired, like I had the flu. She stole my Cookielicious Crunch and laughed when I tried to get it back, so I tried some of her eggs. They were dry: bad trade.

The camp smell was so foul, I almost gagged. No one else seemed bothered.

"You do pranks, Arish?" asked Jo, giving me back my cereal. "My aunt and uncle would kill me if I tried."

"Oh yeah," said Arish. "I'm a prank master! One time during the twins' birthday, I filled a bunch of balloons with glitter and confetti and set them up so when the twins came through the door, the balloons popped all over them!"

Eddy picked up a piece of bacon, setting Bombshell beside his plate. "That sounds terrible."

"It was," said Arish cheerfully. "I got grounded. I spent hours picking up little bits of paper before my parents allowed me to vacuum. And my clothes had glitter on them for weeks! Totally worth it, though."

Jo laughed. "I bet!"

It might not have been a good night's sleep, but Jo was clearly feeling better. Both Counselor Molly and Bethany were in bed when Jo and I had snuck back, so that was lucky. Unlike Jo, though, I'd tossed and turned, thinking about what had happened.

Good Guy George shuffled behind me, lifting a mug over my head as he squeezed between me and the next table. "Ope, good morning." He sipped his coffee before wrinkling his nose and lowering his mug onto the table. "Glad to see everyone behaving this morning."

"We don't want to get kicked out," said Eddy, slouching as he played with his food.

"We're perfect angels," said Jo.

George nodded and wagged a finger. "Be safe now,

ya hear? Don't let me catch you out of bed!"

He left without taking his coffee.

Arish leaned forward. "Too bad about the Glade, though. It was super cool."

"But dangerous," reminded Eddy. "Didn't you see Pina's cut? It's better this way."

I gnawed on my lower lip and clicked my spoon against the bottom of my empty bowl. "I—"

"Stop that," snapped Jo. "That's annoying."

"Oh, sorry." I let go of the bowl.

She scowled. "Stop saying sorry for everything. You always do that! Like you're sorry for breathing. I mean, sheesh, can you not?"

I flinched. Jo had never gotten angry with me before. At least, not until yesterday, when she told me she was moving.

"Khoobee?" I asked.

She . . . *glared* at me.

Eddy's brows furrowed. "Jo, it's not a big deal."

"It *is* a big deal!" Jo shook her head wildly, her short hair whipping around her head. "You don't get it. You're not with her 24–7."

My worst fears—that Jo would leave me forever, that

she was sick and tired of what a fraidy-cat I was, that I annoyed her by being too needy—were coming true. I swallowed a whimper. Jo knew I was useless. Jo was finally mad at me for being her shadow. But I couldn't lose her, not now, not a month before she moved to another state.

I started to apologize again but cut myself off. That would make her madder. Instead, I mumbled, "We're not going to be together once you move."

"And good riddance!" She slammed her fists onto the table. "All you do is hide behind me like a big baby! You need me to hold your hand through everything!"

I'd messed this up somehow. I'd ruined our friendship. How was I going to survive without Jo? With her *hating* me?

I clenched my fists. She was right; I couldn't do anything without her. But I'd helped fight a spider army and gotten around Ms. Angela and pulled Jo back from across the river. I might not be Pina 2.0 yet, but I was at least Pina 1.5.

"Don't listen to them, Pina," said Arish. "That's mean, Jo."

"Mean? *Mean?*" She laughed a laugh that didn't sound like hers. "What's mean is making me responsible for her!

What's mean is making me babysit her constantly! What's mean is itsy-bitsy Pina not being able to do anything without me around!"

The words smacked me in the gut.

Itsy-bitsy Pina, fly away home. Play by yourself and die in the loam.

A smell like manure rose from the table as Jo's ears turned darker and darker red. The more she yelled, the more intense the smell got. Each of our dishes materialized bubbling yellow-green goo, the color of the Glade's glow. Eddy yelped and shoved his plate. My pulse quickened in my throat as I stared at Jo's eggs. The goo swirled like the fountain of spiders from my nightmare the first night at camp, and brown and gray mushrooms wiggled free.

Arish's jaw dropped. Eddy looked as sick as I felt. Jo's chest heaved.

Something was *very* wrong.

"What's this shouting?" demanded an adult voice. Footsteps clomped behind us. My heartbeat galloped four hundred miles an hour as Ms. Angela stomped up to the table. She had on Mom Look #11, *Stern*. "What's this hubbub? Why are you yelling this early in the morning?

You're disrupting breakfast!" If Ms. Angela could smell the nasty mushrooms, she didn't show it—but I swore she looked at our plates a beat too long.

Jo peered up at Ms. Angela and smiled. "Angela."

Ms. Angela crossed her arms. "There's no need to shout. You've gotten everyone riled up. What kind of troublemaker are you? Come, now. If you're going to behave like you need a time-out, then that's what you're getting."

Time-out? We weren't little kids anymore. And the word "troublemaker" was one Jo heard a lot from our teachers and her guardians. She hated it.

But the anger on Jo's face was replaced with a serene smile as she followed Ms. Angela out of the cafeteria, leaving behind her stinky plate.

"What in the heck?" Arish scratched his head. He pushed around his food. "Wow, this stuff looks gnarly. Cool!"

"Dude, not the time," said Eddy. "Something is seriously wrong with Jo. That was *not* normal."

"Is everything okay?" Kiki had come over. A few tables behind them sat Constance and Mackenzie, both looking concerned. Bethany's gang was also at the table, heads bent, glancing our way and giggling.

"Fine!" My voice was too loud. I scraped our gross food into my empty bowl and went to dump it out, but Kiki hadn't moved when I got back. I scrambled to come up with an excuse and was surprised when Arish said Jo had hidden being sick and had to be convinced to rest. After Kiki left, Eddy looked impressed. Arish told him he was used to thinking on his feet.

Kiki caring enough to check in, even though we hadn't hung out much lately, reminded me that I couldn't help Jo alone. The invisible force that had tried to take Jo away was powerful—powerful enough, it seemed, to influence her outside the Glade.

"I have to tell you guys something," I said.

I explained how Jo had been acting weird yesterday, without sharing our private conversation, and jumped ahead to waking up in the middle of the night and what had happened in the Glade.

"There was one more strange thing."

"You mean besides *everything*?" said Arish.

Eddy elbowed him. "Not helping! Go on, Pina."

I smiled a not-smile and traced the squiggles on the table. "You remember when Jo went across the river the first time, and I wasn't there? I'd found another stem-trunk.

THE GLADE

This one looked super old. It was covered in vines and mushrooms. Jo's door last night was starting to look like it."

Eddy's eyes widened. "What do you think that means?"

This was it: time to share the conclusion I'd drawn last night. "You remember that kid who went missing? And how George said he thought someone was calling to him down there? I've been hearing that too, and it usually speaks in freaky nursery rhymes. And George mentioned that his friend acted weird after probably visiting the Glade. So what if . . . what if the kid *didn't* go missing? What if they got trapped in the Glade instead, and they're trying to come back through Jo?" I dug my nails into my thighs. My throat was so, so dry, I almost picked up George's abandoned coffee. "Does that sound impossible?"

"You're the scientist." Arish shrugged. "If you think that's what happened, I believe it."

"Me too," said Eddy. "It makes sense, based on what you've said."

Warmth filled my chest and belly. Neither of them had hesitated, trusting me immediately, but this wasn't the time to get emotional. "I can't know for sure, but it fits what we know."

A scientist had to collect data for any conclusion. Between what George knew and my own observations, plus everything scientists didn't yet understand about mycelium networks—if that's what we were dealing with—I had no idea what was possible. But I did know this: one, Jo had been drawn past what seemed to be safe (or, at least, known) in the world below; two, what happened in the Glade affected our waking bodies; and three, something or someone else was also in the Glade, and it—they—wanted Jo.

"We need to learn more," said Eddy. "About the Glade and about the kid. Do you think there's something online we could find?"

"There's no Wi-Fi," said Arish. "Some of the others were complaining about it."

"But Ms. Angela has an office," I said, thinking aloud. "And a computer. We could sneak in and use it." I'd broken more rules over this last week-plus than my whole life, but to save Jo, we had no choice.

Arish and Eddy glanced at each other, then back at me. Arish grinned. "Time to be a supersecret spy!" He flicked his signature glasses over his eyes.

Eddy's forehead scrunched, but he nodded. "It's our best bet. What if she has a password?"

THE GLADE

"She has a bunch of sticky notes all over her computer," I recalled. "I bet one of them has the password on it. My mom does that with her laptop."

"Why have a password if you're gonna write it down for anyone to see?" Arish bounced in his seat. "This is gonna be awesome. I'm psyched."

"Calm down," said Eddy. "Let's not get caught before we get started."

We spent the rest of the day, whenever we weren't broken into our groups, figuring out the details of our plan. What we'd need to research, and where we might look.

Jo didn't come back.

When it was close to lights-out, I went to brush my teeth. We were going to wait a few hours until the counselors—and Ms. Angela—were asleep.

Mint flavor filled my mouth as I brushed. When I spat out the toothpaste, I must have swallowed some, because my throat itched. I spat again before I realized something was *in* my throat. No, wait. Something was in my *windpipe*, the airway that led to my lungs!

For a moment I couldn't breathe. I coughed, and the thing shifted. I kept coughing, spit flying everywhere. Trying not to panic, I gripped the edges of the sink, spots peppering my vision. Was I going to throw up? Was I choking on nothing and going to die?

Another cough pushed whatever it was higher. I leaned over, shoving my chest into the sink, and held the cough until my throat burned. At last, the slimy object slipped onto my tongue, and I spat it out.

At the bottom of the sink was a big, sticky mushroom.

THIRTEEN

"Be quiet," I scolded Arish as we snuck toward Ms. Angela's cabin. Once everyone was asleep, I'd slipped out to meet the boys.

"How you gonna be a spy when you're so loud?" complained Eddy, also keeping his voice low.

It sounded like Arish had snapped every twig in existence. "Sorry," he said in his loud whisper. "They're booby traps!"

Eddy sighed.

When we got to Ms. Angela's cabin, we headed to the back garden. It was overgrown and wild. The lettuce was huge, and a million tiny tomatoes sagged on their vines. The *Delphinium* and *Echinacea* and Shasta daisies opened wide.

But the garden smelled like stinky cheese and compost, the same smell as the mushrooms Jo had created in our breakfast. A more intense version of the lingering camp smell.

Arish yelped and clapped a hand over his mouth. He'd scratched himself on a thorny vine, which wrapped around the back door handle. The vines covered everything, twisting around the stems of the flowers, sticking out of the dirt.

Mushrooms wiggled next to them.

"The door's locked," said Arish.

Eddy held up a fake-looking rock. "Found the key." He turned it upside down and opened the compartment underneath. We'd been right about the spare key; he and Arish had taken turns following the counselors coming here and had seen them go through the back when Ms. Angela was in the Rec Hall.

Arish unlocked the door, avoiding the vines. When he pushed it open, it creaked. We froze.

No one came out. We tiptoed inside, and Arish quietly shut the door behind us. Not wanting to risk someone seeing the office lights, the boys pulled out their flashlights. Arish, the tallest without Jo here, looked through the bookcase.

I wished Jo were here.

This was no time to wallow; I had a job to do. Eddy searched through Ms. Angela's drawers as I shuffled the sticky notes until I found one that read *cH@r1iE*. Charlie?

The computer was in sleep mode, and the password got me in. I sat in the big chair as I opened the internet browser to search. Meanwhile, Eddy pulled out a file to read, and Arish pulled down books.

The first hit under *Camp Clear Skies* was the official website. I opened it, but not surprisingly, the ABOUT US section didn't have anything useful.

My other searches were more specific—about the camp's history but also for any missing kids, ghost stories, or urban legends in the area. I started to read after I'd opened a handful of promising websites.

Local news stories covered the camp's reopening, some mentioning the previous camp without details. Local legends mostly involved bigfoot or other unprovable cryptids, like George had mentioned. I did find one blog that talked about the Glade, but not by name, calling it a "mystical site in the woods" where "dreams came true."

More like nightmares.

In the bottom corner of the shelves, Arish found children's books: Mother Goose stories, fairy tales, and nursery rhymes. The initials C. D. were written inside every cover.

C. D. Hmm. The few markings left on the abandoned stem-trunk had felt like a *D*, but there'd been an *S*, not a *C*.

"No secret lair or anything," Arish said at almost his usual volume, "but you said you were hearing nursery rhymes, Pina."

Eddy and I shushed him.

Sticking his tongue out at us, Arish paged through one of the books, and a single photograph fell out: an older and younger pair of kids with strawberry blond hair and lots of freckles, holding up sticks with toasted marshmallows. They looked familiar. I frowned until Eddy said, "Those are the same people in the picture from Ms. Angela's kitchen! Remember, Pina?"

That jogged my memory. We'd thought it might be

Ms. Angela and a sibling. Arish flipped over the photo, which was dated about twenty-five years ago. They were clearly younger in this photo than the other.

With the books a bust, Arish joined me at the computer. "What's that one?" He pointed to one of the tabs I hadn't read yet. I switched over to it.

CAMP CLEAR SKIES: A SORDID HISTORY

> *The early 2000s was a time of hope. After surviving Y2K and ushering in the new millennium, so many of us thought we'd have bright futures ahead, having no idea what awaited us.*

"What's Y2K?" asked Arish.

I waved him off and scrolled, looking for something more useful. "Oh! Here!"

> *Long have rumors surrounded why the old camp closed. But I was there the day they called our parents to pick us up, so I can share a firsthand account of what happened.*

One day the head of the camp gathered everyone at the fire pit and told us there'd been an emergency and that the camp was shutting early. No one knew who had gotten hurt or gone missing. The counselors were tight-lipped.

Only later did we learn the truth: one of the campers had gotten sick and fallen into a coma. His name was Charlie. Charlie and I were in the same age group, so we'd spent the weeks hiking, swimming, and playing games. He was a nice kid who knew every nursery rhyme in existence. I especially remember him because he said his favorite food was mushrooms, which was strange for an eleven-year-old.

"Charlie." I glanced back at the sticky note with the computer password.

Something banged outside. Then came scratches. None of us moved until the noises stopped. Had it been an animal, or—no, it must have been. If we'd been caught, they'd have come inside. Right?

"I found something!" Eddy whispered. The open

folder on the desk had a bunch of yellowing brochures. The camp mentioned wasn't named Clear Skies, but based on the pictures, it was definitely the same place. He pushed them aside. "Look, there are a ton of newspaper articles!"

"Who reads newspapers nowadays?" asked Arish.

"I think old people. My grandpa does." I picked up one of the clippings.

The articles were about Charles Douglass, an eleven-year-old who'd gone to camp and fallen into a coma. As the dates went on, the articles got smaller and smaller, until one several months later was only a few lines long, saying doctors weren't hopeful about him waking up.

"A coma, huh?" I added this evidence to my data pool. Douglass—*D* and *S*, like on the stem-trunk. "When we're in the Glade, our bodies are lying there, right?"

Arish whistled under his breath. "You were right, Pina. He must have crossed the river and not gotten out."

"Wait a minute," said Eddy. "Douglass . . . I know that name. I read it in—"

The light flicked on.

I covered my eyes, blinking to adjust my vision. My heart dropped into my belly. We'd been caught.

Ms. Angela stood at the door. "Clever kids. I thought you might sneak out again, but breaking into my office? My, my." She didn't sound mad. She wasn't even wearing an angry Mom Look; she was smiling. She closed the office door behind her and rested against it. "Now, what to do with you?"

"Your brother." Eddy's hand shook as he held up the photograph. "The kid who fell into a coma. That was your brother."

"My little brother," she agreed.

"What did you do?" My stomach was going to vomit out my mouth at this rate.

Ms. Angela spread her arms. "Why, all this, of course." She probably didn't mean the office.

"Are you some sort of supervillain?" demanded Arish. "What's the point of opening up the camp again?"

Ms. Angela chuckled. "Would a villain make so many children happy? Haven't you had fun here at Camp Clear Skies?" She paused. "And the Glade?"

Arish gaped at her, but Eddy hung his head as if he'd been expecting that. I hugged myself, trying not to shake. "You know about the Glade?"

"Of course I know about the Glade." She scoffed.

THE GLADE

"I knew that's where you kids were sneaking off to, like we did decades ago. You think I didn't see you scurrying out of the woods like insects? Sticks and stones may make some groans, but noises didn't hide you."

I rubbed my sweaty palms on my shorts. I hadn't saved us that day after all. "And you let us? You knew we were sneaking out, and you didn't care?"

"Oh, I cared, but not about that." Angela walked up to the desk, picking up the picture Eddy had found. Her smile was sad. "Charlie loved the Glade. He had a hard time making friends, and I was several years older, so he often kept himself busy. When he found the Glade, he was so excited to show me. It became our secret place, where I didn't feel like I had to pretend he annoyed me to prove something to my so-called friends, and he could be himself. One day he went exploring alone, and that was the last time my brother's body woke up."

"You could have gone after him," I said.

"You think I didn't try? They moved his body before I could get to it, and then they shut down the camp."

"Why didn't you tell your parents?" To be fair, I hadn't exactly called my mom to tell her about Jo, either.

"My *parents*," sneered Ms. Angela, her eyes flashing

and lips snarling. It was the first time she seemed truly angry, beyond the anger of Mom Look #8. "The accident destroyed them and my family with it. My mother cried herself to sleep every night. My father stopped coming home. They were never the same. They divorced a year later. They abandoned me, and worse than that, they abandoned *him*. At the time I naively thought that if I could bring Charlie back, then my family would be fixed. I took his body out of our house and brought him back here."

Eddy's eyes widened before he looked away. His parents were divorced too, and he didn't feel like he'd been enough. Ms. Angela had lived Eddy's worst nightmare.

"Your parents let you take him?" Arish asked. "Why wasn't he in the hospital?"

"He was there at first, but my parents didn't believe doctors could help him." Angela shrugged. "Not like it mattered to them where Charlie was. After my father left, my mother would lock herself in her room for days at a time. She didn't notice when I took him, but my plan didn't work. I tried calling him back from across the river, but it was too late—he'd been apart from his body for too long. And then I grew older, and it was clear that even if his mind could return, he'd never wake up."

"So, what?" said Arish. "You bought the camp and opened it back up to find someone younger for him to possess?"

"Precisely." Ms. Angela's eyes shone in the harsh office light.

"But what about that kid's mind?" asked Eddy, throwing up his hands. "Another family would have to go through what your family did!"

"Isn't it convenient that Charlie found a person whose family wants them gone?" Angela's smile returned. "Or haven't you noticed that not everyone can hear the Glade's summons? A kid has to be desperate to prefer a fantasy world to real life."

I cringed. Did Angela know whatever the Glade knew about us? How did she know about Jo's family? From our talk with George, I remembered my own observation: the Glade spoke to lonely kids.

"Where's Jo?" My voice wobbled. I wanted to cry. I wanted to go home. I wanted my best friend.

Ms. Angela's smile widened. "Oh, I wouldn't worry about her. She'll be in a land of imagination that she can control to match her whims. Much better than our world, wouldn't you say?"

"If you believed that, you wouldn't have done all this to get your brother back." I tightened my self-hug. If I let go, I'd break apart.

"Perhaps." She closed her eyes and swallowed, grimacing, before taking a breath and opening her eyes. "But Charlie deserves to have a chance to live again. That was snatched away from him."

"He was the one who crossed the river!" Arish half shouted.

"And so did Jo," said Ms. Angela. "Because if she hadn't, we wouldn't be here, would we? I made sure to keep an eye on who would be a good candidate. Jo doesn't have a loving family to return to. Charlie has me."

And Jo had *me*.

"One more night should do it, I think." She tapped her chin. "Then Charlie's mind will have transferred over completely. He'll have to get used to such a . . . *different* body, but we'll figure it out. And of course, I can't have you interfering." She gestured to her garden, and when we turned, vines were covering the window before our eyes. "I'll introduce you when the transfer is complete, shall I?"

THE GLADE

She laughed, the high pitch making me wince. "Nighty night, children."

"Wait!" I cried, but she'd already turned off the light and closed the door. A key went into the lock on the other side, and there was a scrape like a chair being dragged across the floor. I jiggled the handle and shoved, but it wouldn't budge.

Arish rushed to the back door, but that wouldn't move either. The scratching from earlier must have been Ms. Angela barring it from the outside—I should have trusted my doubts! With the vines tangled around the window, it'd be impossible to open.

We were trapped.

FOURTEEN

Arish yelled and shook the door handle, running from one door to the other. Neither budged.

"Stop!" shouted Eddy. "You're not helping!"

"We have to do something!" Arish kicked the back door. "No one knows we're here! We'll be trapped unless someone hears us!"

"Then what?" demanded Eddy. "You heard Angela! Jo's almost gone." He began to pace. "This is so messed up. An adult created a camp to put her brother in another kid's body. She's supposed to be responsible for us and had this planned instead." Eddy was breathing hard. "This isn't a movie, Arish. You can't make it better because you say so. We're not superheroes or superspies. We're just kids. I don't even have Bombshell to make me feel better."

Arish looked like he'd dropped a fresh s'more on the grass.

I sank onto the floor by Angela's desk and tucked my knees to my chest. Eddy was right—we were stuck here because the person in charge had tricked us. Soon a stranger would steal Jo's body like she was an outfit to wear, not a human with a life and experiences and feelings of her own.

Oh, Jo. My best friend in the whole world. Who I might lose forever.

This was supposed to be the summer of Pina 2.0. The summer when I'd prove to my mom and dad that I could take care of myself. The summer when Jo wouldn't have to stand up for me anymore. Instead, I wasn't Pina 1.5 or even Pina 1.0 anymore. I was Pina 0.0, stuck in a cabin while my best friend got lost in a mysterious mushroom land.

The boys were quiet, but I could almost hear faraway beeping counting down to our doom. Like our cabins, the office smelled musty. Mom would have talked about her cinnamon spray if she were here.

But she wasn't here. She hadn't wanted me at camp in the first place. Ms. Angela might call our parents and get them to pick us up tomorrow, but it would be too late. Who cared about camp or parents when Jo was in danger?

How hadn't I realized that Jo had been struggling? For as long as we'd been friends, she'd been my rock, and I'd been hers. It didn't matter that my mom and dad were strict. It didn't matter that her aunt and uncle were mean. But until Jo brought it up, I hadn't realized how awful Aunt Lyd and Uncle Brock had been about her dad's family. I thought Jo brushed off whatever they said like she brushed off everything else. I thought it was easier for her because she *didn't* know anything about being Filipino. Baba's family expected me to know what it meant to be Persian, but they laughed whenever I tried. Before our conversation the other night, I'd thought it was nice that Jo didn't have that pressure. Maybe she still wanted to try, even if she got laughed at.

But I had to be honest: it *was* different for Jo. Because Aunt Lyd and Uncle Brock didn't *want* her to connect with her dad's heritage. Jo couldn't pretend she didn't look different from her guardians. At least I could look at a photo of me and my dad and see how I looked like him. Jo didn't get to do that. From what I understood, "Kaya mo ba?" meant something like "Can you do it?" but for Jo, it was more than a phrase—it was her lifeline to a family who would have loved her.

My fingers and toes tingled as I rocked and held back the rising need to barf. My chest felt tight enough to burst. If I'd been stuck in a small space again like the stem-trunk, I'd have let myself melt down. Instead, everything felt caught inside me, and if I didn't let it out, I'd explode.

It was like I hadn't even known my best friend. There were so many things she hadn't shared, but had I asked her about them? Nope. She always took care of me, so wasn't I supposed to always take care of her, too? I thought I *was* taking care of her. Every day after school, Jo and I would go to the library to do homework, and when her guardians didn't get her, she'd come home with me to have dinner. On weekends, if Mom didn't have me doing ten million things, we'd go to the community center to hang out. The only times we didn't see each other were holidays, when we drove up to see Mom's parents.

If Jo felt like she didn't belong anywhere, did those memories mean nothing?

Soon she'd be bound to that make-believe land, and some creep would take over her body—a "real American" kid who could be what Jo couldn't. He probably knew he was a boy, and his parents had wanted him enough to divorce once he was gone. As messed up as it was, he even had a sister who loved him so much, she rebuilt the camp where she'd lost him. He wouldn't go home and hear how his mom had made a mistake to have a baby with "someone like that." He wouldn't go to school and be labeled a troublemaker without giving his side of the story.

He'd get everything Jo never could.

I wished she were here with me. Eddy and Arish were nice, but they weren't Jo. Jo would know exactly what to do or say.

What *would* she say right now? I imagined her sitting next to me. If she were here, she'd have her back against Ms. Angela's desk drawers and twist her cap backward. *What are you moping around for?* she'd say. *You're Dr. Scientist Pina! You're on the case!*

I can't do anything without you, I told her in my head.

That's silly, said Imagined Jo. *You do plenty of things without me. You were the one who argued with your mom to come to camp, and you made yourself a jetpack in the Glade, and you also figured out how the Glade might work!*

Those were good points. I played with my hoodie drawstring. *I wish you were here to tell me what to do.*

P, said the Jo in my head. *I don't tell you what to do. You're the one who's gotten us out of sticky situations. Remember when we almost got caught by Ms. Angela? Or how you dragged me back from across the river?*

That was true. Angela may have seen us that day, but we'd *felt* safe.

I know you can save me, she said. *Because you're Pina, and you think things through and come up with plans no one else would. Since we've come here, you've used that big brain of yours over and over to get us out of trouble. So you'll get me out of trouble too.*

Jo was right.

But I wasn't talking to Jo. I was talking to Imagined Jo, which meant I was talking to . . . myself?

Since I was pretending that Jo was giving me a pep talk, didn't that mean I was actually giving myself one? That meant I could figure this out on my own, because I knew the real Jo believed in me, so I had to believe in me too.

If I could figure out how to escape from here, I could also figure out how to save Jo from Ms. Angela and a kid who never got to grow up.

(The whole thing still felt gross, but I couldn't pinpoint why.)

I wiped my face and palms and stood up. Arish looked at me from where he was lying down on the floor, making not-snow-angels.

"We can't sit here and do nothing," I said. "We have to get out."

"We already tried the doors," said Arish. "We've been captured, and not even by space pirates!"

Eddy and I ignored this.

"Plus, the window's covered." Eddy gestured to the vines that barely let moonlight through.

"There has to be something here." How silly that we were in the dark! I flicked on the light switch by the door and took stock of the room. Back door, main door. A desk with drawers and a computer. Two big bookshelves. "Help me look!"

Eddy stood up. "Look for what?"

"Anything that feels out of place." An idea niggled in

THE GLADE

the back of my mind, but I wasn't sure what it was yet.

Arish got up too, and he and Eddy traded places so Eddy could look at the bookshelves and Arish could look through the desk. I tried the main door again.

I was missing something. I grabbed Arish's jumbo-sized flashlight and searched around the back door. Through the crack I could hear the wind howling. The vines rustled over the window as if looking for a way in.

I could smell it again: the earthy perfume and rotting stink of the mushrooms Jo—or rather, Charlie—had made appear in our breakfast.

If I strained my ears, I could hear something, but what was it?

I went back to the area where I'd been sitting. There it was again—the funk of mushrooms. "Do you guys smell anything?"

Both sniffed and shrugged, but Eddy came over. He frowned. "It smells like the cabins."

Arish came over too. "I don't smell—wait. Do you hear that?"

After a few silent heartbeats, I did: a high-pitched whine. I couldn't tell what it was. Then I heard something else: quiet beeps.

The boys and I looked at one another before we began rooting around where I'd been sitting. Angela's desk drawers were not attached to her desk, and after Arish found the latch stopping the wheels from moving, we rolled them out of the way.

A trapdoor lay underneath.

FIFTEEN

I shined the flashlight into the dark hole of the open trapdoor. The stairs looked rickety at best, and the smell of rotting fruit reeked so much, I gagged.

"This makes me wanna hurl." Sweat beaded on Arish's forehead. "Do we gotta go down there?"

"It's our best shot." Eddy looked nervous too.

I took a deep breath. Jo wasn't here to be brave, so I had to be brave for us. "I'll go first. Can one of you hold the big flashlight for me?" I handed it over to Arish, who gulped and nodded. Eddy handed over his little flashlight for me to pocket.

I climbed down. The whole time, I told myself Jo

wouldn't hesitate to do this to help me. That splinters could be taken out. That spiders could be squashed.

My feet hit the bottom. I released my death grip on the stairs with a shaky breath.

"Pina?" called Arish.

"I made it." I turned Eddy's flashlight onto the room.

I first noticed the vines and mushrooms. It was impossible not to. The mushrooms gleamed yellow green like in the Glade, hanging from the ceiling, poking up from the floor, sticking out of the walls. The vines running alongside were as thick as my arm, and thorns cast shadows from the glow.

Most of the growth was wrapped around a setup in the middle of the room. The focus was a bed, its front half bent up and a bunch of equipment around it. As I shined the flashlight, I wanted to hurry back up the ladder.

There was a *person* lying on the bed.

A thump sounded behind me. Arish peered over my shoulder. "Holy . . . !"

Eddy came around my other side. "Wow. It looks kind of like a hospital room. My mom's a doctor, but I've never seen an at-home room in a basement."

"I don't think any of us have seen anything like this

before, Eddy-spaghetti." Arish wasn't smiling.

The beeping I'd heard earlier was from a screen hooked up to the person, which, according to the movies, measured the person's heartbeat. The high buzzing Arish had heard came from the equipment too. Vines wrapped around the monitors and wires like they were supposed to be there.

Eddy picked up yellow papers from a box on the ground. He coughed as dust puffed up from the sheets, then tilted them toward the glow to read. I stepped closer to the bed, my flashlight shaking.

Mushrooms covered the person's body—no, not just a person: a kid. Orange stalks pushed up from their belly, tearing through the hospital gown. Brown blooms dotted their forehead like giant warts. Their frail fingers had little caps instead of nails. The smell was worse than rotting fruit—like spoiled milk and old meat.

I shuddered. They didn't look human anymore.

"It's Charlie." Eddy pressed his lips together. "I guess Angela hasn't let doctors look at him for a long time. There's a bunch of insurance hocus-pocus in here about it. She must have relocated him here when she set up the camp."

"Hard to explain why your brother in a coma hasn't aged," said Arish.

We looked at the unmoving figure. Not unmoving—a vine curled around a finger. A mushroom vibrated. Almost like they were also medical equipment.

"This is seriously messed up," said Arish.

"For real," said Eddy. "My gramma says white people like taking things and claiming credit like they invented or discovered them. This feels kinda like that for some reason."

Something like pity or disgust settled in my gut. Charlie's mind had been stuck in the Glade for a very, very long time, so long that his body looked like his stem-trunk and hadn't aged, a snapshot of a lost childhood.

Angela had said his mind and body had been apart for too long, which meant that even if his body was in the clearing, that might not be enough to call his mind out of Jo's. But maybe we could do something about the place that linked him and Jo together.

"I have an idea," I said.

We wouldn't have noticed the back door if we hadn't been looking for it. Eddy was the one who saw the rusty handle. Arish took the trapdoor stairs back to Ms. Angela's office and returned with a pair of scissors. If this were the Glade, I could have imagined myself with a sword. But it wasn't, so instead, we took turns sawing the vines until Arish slammed into the door hard enough for it to open.

Air blasted into the creepy basement, a welcoming change despite the usual odor. We gulped in fresh air and climbed over the rest of the vines to squeeze through what was actually a root cellar entrance. Long thorns tore at our clothes, but we didn't care. We had to get help, and fast, before Jo was lost forever.

The converted root cellar opened into Ms. Angela's garden. We didn't bother to be careful as we ran through. Vines held big wooden planks over the back office door.

More vines snaked toward us. Arish yelped and stomped on one that grabbed Eddy's ankle.

We weren't in the Glade to use our superpowers, so when we escaped the garden, I counted us lucky.

"Ah *ha*!" shrieked a familiar voice. I groaned as we saw Mean Girl Bethany stomping toward us. Her hair was pulled back like usual, but she wore a fluffy robe. What kid used a bathrobe? "I *knew* you were out making trouble again! You're going to get kicked out for *sure*. Breaking into Ms. Angela's cabin!"

"More like breaking out," said Arish.

"We have bigger problems." My anger surprised me, though it probably shouldn't have. "Angela's got Jo! We don't have time for this!"

Bethany scowled. "Ex*cuse* me? That's *Ms*. Angela to you. What's this nonsense you're spouting?" She said it how Angela might.

We shared the highlights of what had happened, but Bethany looked skeptical.

"We're telling the truth," said Arish. "You gotta help us!"

"Ms. Angela is a strong, independent woman," said Bethany with a sniff. "She got the place up and running after years and years. Jealousy is ugly."

She thought we were jealous of Ms. Angela? My head hurt.

"Even if I did believe you—which I don't—it's not like I can do anything," Bethany added. "Only my dork brother has the 'authority.'"

"Great," I said. "Can someone get him?"

"What?" said Bethany. "Why?"

"We need him. Eddy, he'll take you more seriously than Arish—"

"Hey!"

"Get over it, Arish, she's right," said Eddy. "Wait for me." He ran off.

Arish and I led Bethany back through the garden, which behaved since we were returning. Bethany took Arish's flashlight to climb inside the disturbing basement.

After what felt like the longest minutes of my life, Bethany returned. Her eyes glinted, almost like they were glowing too. "Well, well, well. This is some twisted research. I can't wait to tell Daddy! Angela's in deep. No wonder she's been asking so much about you."

"What?" demanded Arish. "You were spying on us for Ms. Angela?"

"I was being responsible." Bethany turned up her nose. "Nothing wrong with that!"

Typical.

"Fer cripes' sake," came a grumble. Eddy returned with George, who looked sleepy but had managed to grab his trusty orange fanny pack. George's eyes widened as he looked around. "This glow . . . it looks like—"

"The Glade," said Eddy. "Like I told you. We have to rescue Jo before it's too late."

I nodded. "He's right. We need your help."

George straightened. "Because I understand the Glade?"

"Sure." I shrugged. "Also, you have the Rec Hall keys."

SIXTEEN

The Glade's clearing was glowing when we reached it. Like I'd expected, Ms. Angela and Jo were both already there. Angela had brought a pillow and sleeping bag, but Jo lay on the ground without anything else, wearing her same T-shirt and shorts from this morning.

I recited every Farsi word I knew so I wouldn't start crying. I was scared, and I was tired, and I wanted this to be over.

Arish hefted one of the buckets we'd brought, water sloshing out of it. George had the other, and Bethany carried a box of backup supplies.

"Are you sure you want to go in alone?" asked Eddy, juggling four thermoses of coffee to help them stay awake.

I nodded. "It's safer this way. Remember the plan. Start as soon as I'm asleep. We don't know how much time we have." We'd gone over my idea as we gathered supplies, with George pitching helpful suggestions and Bethany pitching bad ones.

"You're so cool, Pina," said Arish, his face serious. "I'm so scared, I could pee my pants!"

"Oh my God." Bethany dropped her box and swiped a thermos from Eddy. "Do *not* pee your pants. I can*not* deal with that right now."

I ignored their bickering and lay down next to Jo, as far away from Angela as I could. I took Jo's hand and threaded our fingers together. Hers were cold and lifeless.

"I'm coming, Jo," I whispered, pressing my face into the crook of her neck, and waited for the perfume of the Glade to kick in.

When I opened my eyes, I was in my stem-trunk. I shoved forward, expecting Jo—or, more accurately, Charlie in Jo's body—to have blocked it again, but it flew open. I stumbled through, falling on my hands and knees.

"Proserpina."

I froze.

Mom and Baba stood on the lichen-moss in front of my stem-trunk, arms crossed as they looked down at me. Mom wore Mom Look #1; she was *not* going to argue with me.

"What are you doing here?" she demanded. "You should be in camp! I knew it was a mistake to let you go in the first place. I thought I was teaching you independence, but you're running around on some dangerous and ridiculous errand!"

"Baba-jaan." My dad shook his head. "We expected better of you. You were supposed to follow the rules. We thought we could trust you." A wriggling black mass the size of a dime snaked down from his nostril. He sniffed it up.

I shrank back. "I—"

"No excuses!" A spider the size of my hand crawled up my mom's shoulder. "We are so disappointed in you. This silly camp has put all sorts of nonsense in your head. I won't let you out of my sight once you're home! And I won't let you in the garden!"

If I'd been standing, my legs would have given out. Mom would never use the garden as punishment. It was something she and my dad had agreed on—no matter what, even when I was grounded, I'd be allowed to garden.

"Proserpina," said Mom again, but her voice was distorting.

I dug my nails into my palms. "You're not my real parents," I told the Glade. "And even if you were, I'm not doing anything wrong. I'm here to save Jo."

"By yourself?" Not-Mom's voice sounded auto-tuned. "Little, scared Pina, afraid of spiders?"

Another spider crawled up her wrist.

"Itsy-bitsy Pina," said Not-Baba, his voice high-pitched like he'd sucked helium from a balloon, "climbing way too far. Climb any higher, and you might get a scar."

"Itsy-bitsy Pina, oh so small and meek," said Not-Mom. "All by yourself: pathetic, sad, and weak."

"Not by myself." I staggered onto my feet. "My friends helping me doesn't make me small and weak. I'm down here alone, aren't I?"

Not alone. Jo was here.

My shoulders heaved. I could manifest my weapons, but I didn't want to. These might not be my actual parents, but they looked like them.

THE GLADE

"You are *not* my parents," I repeated. "And I won't let you stop me from saving my best friend!"

Howling, I charged, determined to knock them down like a bowling ball did pins.

But my fake parents vanished in an orange puff as I dashed forward. I stumbled but caught myself, turning around. Nothing but my stem-trunk was behind me.

I'd done it.

Not the time to celebrate yet. My jetpack slid onto my shoulders, and I flew as high as I could to look for the river. When I found it, I zoomed over until I hit that spike of pressure. This time I landed before the pressure overwhelmed me and jogged to the riverbank, trying to catch my breath.

Ms. Angela was facing the river when I arrived. Across the bank from the two of us stood Jo.

"Oh no you don't," snapped Angela when she noticed me. She backed up onto the rickety bridge Jo (or Charlie) must have manifested, facing me. "You may have gotten this far, but you shall not pass!"

The fog from last time descended, but rather than the dark swirling gray that had probably been Charlie trying to stop me, this was an orange haze like sunset. It pressed in on me, filling my lungs and chest. I coughed like I had last night with the nasty mushroom, as if that could eject the substance, but it was no use.

My brain felt like it had leaked out of my ears. I needed to escape, but no ideas came to me. The fog slithered over my skin, leaving behind an oily residue that raised the hairs on my body.

Or maybe that was from the dark shape in front of me, stepping closer and closer until it parted the orange smoke.

It was a spider the size of a Great Dane but twice as wide, though it wasn't a *spider* spider. Instead of a fuzzy head with too many eyes, there were eight human heads bunched in a circle on its back. Well, they were shaped like human heads, but the skin was covered in little spider hairs, and there were clusters of eyes where there should have been two, and there were no noses, and the mouths were open black voids. Spindly spider legs burst out of the chittering mouths, as if whole tarantulas would crawl out. Mushrooms sprouted on top of the heads, oozing yellow-green goo.

The big, thick legs holding the creature skittered toward me.

THE GLADE

Screams erupted around us. I realized they were mine when I slammed hard enough onto the ground to knock the wind out of me. Angela had created a beast so horrifying, I would never have been able to imagine it with words, let alone bring it into existence.

The creature overshot as it passed. I rolled over to keep it in my sights. There was no time to panic and shut down as the arachnid nightmare attacked. I dodged again, trying to think of a plan. What could distract or destroy this monster? I was a fly, and it was only a matter of time before I got caught in its web.

Which gave me an idea.

When the mutant terror reared again, I ran around it as fast as I could so that it charged toward the spot where I used to be. At the same time a low buzz grew from underground. The fog swirled as the earth trembled and cracked. A sphere the size of a truck tire rose, and two wings fanned out, vibrating too fast to see. The buzzing roared.

The spider lolled its heads to follow the bait.

With the monster distracted, I manifested my sword and swung at it—once, twice, three times—hacking until the fog swallowed up the spider where it had collapsed.

Panting, I looked over at Angela, who had crossed to

the other side of the river but remained standing on the bridge. She pursed her lips in a *not bad* expression.

"Got through that too, did you? Guess I have to deal with you myself." She held out her hand, and a glow filled it until she also held a sword. "Don't forget, I'm quite well-versed in the tricks of the Glade."

Spiders couldn't stop me, and scary nursery rhymes couldn't stop me, and my fake parents couldn't stop me. Ms. Angela wouldn't stop me either.

I clasped my sword in both hands.

We ran at each other and met in the middle of the wooden crossing. Our weapons clanged and shock rippled through my arms. We bounced back and attacked again. Angela was bigger and stronger than me, but I could weave around her swings despite the unstable shakes of the bridge. Every violent sway made my stomach swoop.

This was taking too long.

I dashed off the bridge, back to my original side. This lured Angela over, so I powered on my jetpack to zoom around her, determined to push through any atmospheric resistance to cross. Before I could, an icy cord snagged my ankle.

I crashed down. Angela held a whip in her hand like

THE GLADE

the movie archaeologist California Jones. She released my ankle and cracked the whip.

I needed a different plan.

We circled each other. When Angela charged, I activated my jetpack again to jump away from her—but not toward the bridge. This time I pointed myself toward the nearby mushroom forest. The forest was crowded, but I had no choice except to trust my instincts to guide me through.

Angela stalked me. She didn't bother with a jetpack of her own; she leapt, her legs stretching like she was made of putty to cover the distance. I managed to catch her in manifested quicksand, but her whip wrapped around a branch to pull herself out.

I had only one shot to get this right, so I zipped up ahead, hoping the quicksand bought me enough time.

When she broke through the not-trees, she growled like a wild animal. "Nowhere else to run," she panted. "You're mine!"

She lunged at me. At the last second I did a somersault in the air; Angela tripped on the big root I'd grown and went sprawling—right into the abandoned and ancient stem-trunk that had been her brother's.

I slammed the door, its vines that I'd hacked away now dangling, and leaned against it to catch my breath. I'd done it. If the others had managed their part in time, Angela was trapped.

Time to get Jo.

SEVENTEEN

Jo was on the other side of the riverbank where I'd seen her last. The bridge Angela and I had fought on remained, looking only a little less unstable with very familiar vines wrapped around it. Not that they'd done much to keep the structure steady during our sword fight.

Tendrils wove around my feet as I stepped onto the bridge, but I shook them off. Unlike when we'd been in Ms. Angela's garden, the vines didn't try to stop me.

My vision swum; I blinked, trying to shake off the sudden dizziness. Was I too late?

I couldn't think like that, not when I was so close. So

I focused, crossed the bridge, and ran toward Jo, who was standing farther away from the river than before.

"Jo!" I yelled. "Jo, you gotta snap out of it! He's gonna trap you here if you don't!"

Jo didn't seem to be getting any closer. With every step I took, the distance between us stretched. She wouldn't turn, even as I kept shouting.

Itsy-bitsy Pina, in the Glade to roam, sang the voice I'd come to expect. *Now she'll turn around and leave us alone. They're almost mine—then I'll go home!*

"No." I tried to sound firm. "You think I'm weak? You think I'm scared? Well, I'm still here, and I won't let you take her without a fight!"

Jo—Not-Jo?—turned around. Vines twisted around her arms and legs, snaking around her like veins. Her fingernails looked painted, but I had a feeling that's not what I'd see up close.

On each of her shoulders sprouted two wrinkled, brain-looking mushrooms—poisonous beefsteak false morels, *Gyromitra esculenta*. It made me think of a Persian myth my dad told me about an evil king with snakes on his shoulders. On top of the mushrooms were tarantulas that raised their abdomens as if to flick those spiky hairs in defense.

THE GLADE

This wasn't Jo. This was Ms. Angela's brother, Charlie, possessing Jo.

I blinked, and Charlie-Jo was no longer in front of me. I turned to see them at the foot of the bridge. They grinned at me, but it wasn't Jo's normal grin. This one had yellow-and-red teeth with white lips stretching way, way too wide.

I blinked again, and Charlie-Jo appeared across the bridge, on the Glade's "normal" side. My jetpack sputtered when I tried to use it; Charlie must have learned from my trick last time. I ran after them as they skipped down the field of lichen-moss, the orange and blue making my head spin.

When I followed across the river, I tried my jetpack again, and it worked. At full throttle, I flew toward Charlie-Jo, but they were fast. One moment they were skipping; the next they were by my stem-trunk, laughing.

Now, now, said Charlie-Jo, their white lips stretched wide open, their mouth ajar without sound coming out. They shook their finger, and then aimed that finger like a gun at my stem-trunk. I hovered, uncertain.

"Jo—"

Wrong! said Charlie-Jo before firing their finger gun.

Flames shot out, torching my stem-trunk.

"No!" My jetpack and sword disappeared. I crashed to the ground, crawling toward my way home. The heat of the blaze wouldn't let me get close. Trying not to cry, I watched the fire rise higher and higher, into the clouds. My door, with those amazing books and plants, up in smoke.

How would I get back to the world above?

I win! Charlie-Jo's lips moved, but the sound was in my head, mismatched with the movement. *Since you like it here so much, I guess you can stay forever!*

Gray goop spilled out of their mouth. It splattered on the ground, and a bright orange mushroom—fool's conecap, *Conocybe filaris*, one of the deadliest—sprouted from it. It smelled like the worst of the above-world smells, rotten fruit and spoiled milk and bad meat and vomit. The goop picked up speed as it spread toward me.

A thick, hairy spider leg oozed out.

Charlie-Jo cackled. Another gooey mushroom dropped from their mouth. A spider crawled out from their tongue. I gagged.

It started to rain.

What the— Charlie-Jo slapped at nothing, then hissed. *What is this?*

THE GLADE

The goop stopped moving, steaming where the rain touched it. I cupped my palms and let the drops pool. The liquid was clear but reddish brown.

The plan. It was working!

I pushed myself up. The rain wasn't hurting me, but Charlie-Jo screamed and thrashed, as if that would help.

It was time to put an end to this.

"Jo!" I called. "You are my best friend in the whole world! You are my family, and I'm your family! Aunt Lyd and Uncle Brock might not love you, but I will *always* love you and never leave you behind!"

Before I could overthink, I charged at Charlie-Jo like I had my fake parents. But instead of going through a puff of smoke, I smashed into their chest, sending the two of us flying.

No. Sending the *three* of us flying.

I rolled onto my knees. Familiar gray fog surrounded me, but I could see silhouettes. A deep inhale left me in a coughing fit. I wheezed, calling Jo's name as I crawled toward the shapes.

"Josephine!" screeched a voice from that direction. "Don't you dare hide from me! Get over here and make yourself useful!"

Another lungful of air had me hacking again. The smell of smoke made my eyes water, but from the sizzling sound, the rain was snuffing out the fire.

"I told your aunt we should have let the State handle you," said a different voice, deep and confident. "Instead, here we are, wasting time and money on some kid we didn't ask for."

"The biggest pain in my butt," sneered Voice #1. "All you do is make trouble!"

A deep, shuddering sigh, on the edge of tears—but not from me. "I know. I'm sorry. I'm not a good kid. I can't do anything right."

Jo! I had to get to her. The rain was slowing down, although the fire hadn't been fully extinguished yet. Crawling to lessen how much smoke I inhaled, I called Jo's name, hoping that she'd hear, that I could reach her.

"We put our lives on hold because of you," snapped Voice #1, Aunt Lyd. "Our plans—gone!"

"I know, I'm sorry you got stuck with me, I'm sorry—"

Jo's voice cracked. I had to hurry.

The silhouettes weren't getting any closer, even though I was moving fast enough to scrape my knees. "Jo, snap out of it! It's not them!" The Glade had amplified the worst parts about my parents, which had to mean Jo was living through the worst parts of her guardians.

"Too bad you're not like Pina," said Aunt Lyd. "Then maybe we'd love you."

A noise tore out of me that I didn't know I could make—an animal howl of rage. Comparing me and Jo was like comparing aspens and lavender: sure, they were both plants, but that's where the similarities stopped.

"DON'T LISTEN TO THEM, JO!"

Everything froze. The swirling smoke—fog, whatever—suspended its patterns. Wary, I coughed and pushed up. The Glade didn't do anything without a reason.

"Pina, huh?" Jo's voice. She chuckled. "You wish I was more like Pina?"

I held my breath. The shapes in the mist dissipated, and her voice came from everywhere.

"You know what Pina does? Pina helps me with my homework instead of telling me I'll never amount to anything, and she shares her lunch and makes sure I eat dinner. Pina takes care of me, unlike *you*!"

Tears raced down my cheeks. Jo knew how much I cared for her, and it *mattered*.

"You know what Pina would say right now? She'd say it's not right that you say such awful things and that I deserve a family who loves me, not people who tear me down every single day. But I don't think being more like her will make you love me. At least Pina accepts me for who I am."

I wiped my face and cheered. "Go, Jo! I'm here for you! You can do it!"

"A family who loves you?" came an unfamiliar voice. "Is that what you want, Josephine?"

I spun on my heel, searching for the source of the new voice, for Jo, for anything through the dense gray curtain that hung around us. It wasn't as thick as it had been, but the coverage was absolute.

When Jo finally spoke, her voice was a whisper. "Mom?"

My blood iced. "It's not her! It's not your mom! It's Charlie! It's the Glade!"

"Ah, Josephine," said the voice. "You don't love your mother, do you?"

"No—wait, Mom, that's not true, I—"

"Because if you did, you'd be better behaved for my sister and her boyfriend. You wouldn't be such a nuisance."

THE GLADE

"Don't listen, Jo!" I shouted again. "It's Charlie! It's the kid trapped in the Glade!"

"Stop it, Mom, please, I'm sorry—"

"You ruined my life," snarled the voice. "If I hadn't had you, I'd never have gotten sick, and I could've lived the perfect life that I was meant to have."

"No! Mom, please, I—"

"I don't want to be your mother."

Sobs echoed around me. Fierce Jo, breaking down into tears. I'd never seen her cry before. My jaw trembled. Jo was nowhere to be seen, and I had no way to reach her, nothing I could use to . . .

Wait. This was the Glade, the place that brought our nightmares to life—and our dreams.

Useless? I was far from useless.

I squeezed my eyes shut to concentrate. So what if Jo was hidden from me? That just meant I had to make sure she could hear me no matter where she was.

A microphone materialized in my hand. Gripping the cool plastic, I took a deep breath and screamed, "JO!"

My call echoed from the speaker floating above the smoke.

"JO!"

"Pina . . . ?"

It was working! "NO!" shrieked a voice that was more auto-tune than Jo's mom. "You're worthless, Josephine! To me and to everyone else! You should have never been born!"

"Jo, listen to me," I urged. The microphone was growing hot—no doubt Charlie's doing. "Do you remember when you found that book with Filipino characters? You ran to me after school and told me about the word 'mabuti.' Kaya mo ba, Jo? Kaya mo ba?"

"Kaya . . . ?"

The hesitation in her voice punched me in the gut. I tossed the microphone from one hand to the other; I wouldn't be able to hold it much longer without burning myself. "I say khoobam when you ask, but now I'm asking you: Kaya mo ba? Khoobee? Kaya mo ba?"

"NO!" wailed Glade Charlie. "NO! You're useless, you're weak, nobody likes you, silly, scared Pina—"

Charlie's words couldn't hurt me anymore, but melting plastic could. The mic sizzled. I dropped it, flapping my hands in pain. "Kaya mo ba?" I yelled. "Kaya mo ba?"

"Mom." Jo's voice, soft. My heart sank. I thought I'd gotten through to her. I thought—

THE GLADE

"You're right, Mom. Your life did change because I was born. And it has been hard on your family because of it."

I shut my eyes. I'd lost her. Charlie had won.

"But that doesn't make it my fault."

My eyes flew open.

"You're my mom, but you haven't acted like one in a long time. You can't take care of yourself or me. And I know you're sick and don't always mean what you say." A deep breath, then: "But being around you hurts me. And I think we should stay separated until you're better. And if that day doesn't come . . . it'll be okay."

The mist around us swirled and drew together, spinning into a globe. Faster and faster, it twirled until all the mist had collected, suspended in midair. Barely a few paces away from me stood Jo. We stared at the hanging ball.

"Goodbye, Mom," said Jo. "Goodbye, lost kid."

The globe began to unravel, shaping itself first into a spider, then a kid, flickering between the shapes as if unsure. It morphed into Glade Charlie's wailing face, stretching as if fighting a powerful wind. A hand reached toward us, but Glade Charlie was flitting between human and spider again, spider and human, his eyes and face morphing into black beads with clicking talons, then back to a scared boy's before he got sucked away, disappearing in the direction of the river and the mushroom forest—and his own stem-trunk, where his sister was trapped.

Jo and I stared at each other. She looked normal again—no more vines, no more mushrooms. She rubbed her eyes, wet and red from crying. "Pina . . . ?"

I gnawed on my lip. Charlie was gone, right? This wasn't a trick? "Kaya mo ba?" Was she okay? Was she back to being my Jo?

She smiled tightly. "Khoobam."

"Jo!" I threw myself at her, and she choked and laughed.

"Easy, easy!" She wrapped her arms around me, pressing her forehead against mine, and I choked back tears.

It was over. Jo was back. Charlie *was* gone.

"You saved me," she marveled. "You—you didn't give up, even when I was mean to you. Well—I don't know if it was him or me, to be honest. You—"

"I love you, Jo." I sniffled. "You'll always be my family. And I didn't save you—*you* saved you. All I did was cheer you on." Reaching with careful fingers, I brushed Jo's hair away from her forehead and wiped the tear streaks on her cheek. "Is it always that bad? With—them?"

Jo sniffed. "No. That was, like . . . the worst times in one go." She pulled back, rubbing her eyes with her palms again. "A lot of times they just . . . say things. Like, Uncle Brock could be watching football and tell me to 'earn my keep' by getting him a beer. Or Aunt Lyd could be clipping coupons and complain about how much food I make us go through. Stuff like that."

If Mom and Baba slipped in comments like those during regular life, not because they were mad or because I'd done something wrong, it would seriously mess me up.

"I'm sorry I didn't notice how bad it was." My hoarse voice wobbled with unshed tears.

"I didn't tell you about any of it."

"I should have asked. I should have put the pieces together. I'm sorry you've been going through this alone."

Jo shook her head. "Not alone. Did you hear me earlier? You took care of me."

I shrugged. It didn't seem like enough.

Jo grabbed my shoulders. "Listen, Pina, I'm sorry about the stuff I said before. I—"

"It's okay," I interrupted. "I know it was Charlie

saying those things. That's Ms. Angela's brother, the kid who possessed you."

Jo bit her lip, taking a half step back before stopping herself to straighten her shoulders and meet my gaze. "He didn't pull those thoughts out of nowhere. It was like he blew up the feelings that I have on bad days and made them the only thing I felt."

A week or two ago, this confession would have hurt my feelings big time. But right now, I felt tired, and after what I'd witnessed, I understood. "It's okay. Sometimes we think not-nice things about people in our lives. I don't think it means we don't care about them."

"But I'm moving." Jo didn't sound irritated, but anxious. "Like, moving for real. That wasn't something I was saying to make you upset. And the stuff about finding a place to belong."

"You will always have a place to belong," I said firmly. "No matter how far you move or how many fights we have, I'll have space for you, just as I know you'll have space for me."

We stood there for however long. I felt okay about Jo not saying anything because I knew, deep down, we'd be okay.

Jo inhaled, held, and exhaled. "Thanks, Pina. Let's get out of . . ."

We both turned to the remains of my stem-trunk—a pile of ash.

"What do we do?" asked Jo. "Can you go home without your trunk?"

I looked around us. The Glade. The first couple of times we came down here were so exciting. A place we built with our imagination. A place where we could be whatever we wanted and learn to be brave.

"I guess it won't be too bad to stay down here." That wasn't true, but I didn't want to make Jo feel worse.

"I am *not* leaving you behind," said Jo. "I'm not leaving without you, period. You rescued me. Now I'll rescue you. We take care of each other, right?"

I smiled a little but shook my head. "I don't want you to do what Ms. Angela tried to do."

Jo frowned. "Me neither. But . . ." She turned to look at the last remaining stem-trunk in the field.

Hers.

"Do we need separate trunks if you're asleep up there?" she asked. "It's just a gateway to the surface."

I gnawed hard on my lip. Angela's trunk was gone—it

must have disappeared when she got trapped in Charlie's. Did that mean anything for her body?

What would happen if I went up with Jo?

She held out a hand. "Ready to go home?"

What if I went in her trunk and got stuck in her body, the way Charlie tried to? Would I disappear, or would we end up sharing?

The thought shook me. I'd never get to see another Mom Look or hear Baba tell me a story. I'd never get bullied for being a nerd. I'd move to Detroit and watch as Jo lived a new life with her guardians. Would I be able to help when they were mean? Or when she felt like an outsider? Would I be able to talk to her and convince her that she belonged?

But I didn't know if that would happen. With so much of the Glade a mystery, sharing a stem-trunk might not mean sharing a body. Sure, if I had to, I'd want it to be with Jo, but after everything we'd been through, together and apart, it would be a bitter victory. Plus, it wouldn't be fair for Jo to have to share her body right after we won it back. There had to be another way to make sure we both made it to the surface together—but separated.

With her hand outstretched, Jo smiled at me, but it

didn't look like her usual Jo smile. Maybe I didn't know her as well as I thought I did, but here's what I did know: to be Pina 2.0, and every version after, I had to be on my own. For Jo to live the life she deserved, so did she.

This wasn't the end. I believed in Jo, and I believed in myself.

As my final act in this world, I manifested her favorite cap—the one I'd given her that had been formerly lost to the Glade—and stuck it on her head backward. "We got this, Jo!"

She laughed for real this time. "All right, P. We got this."

Hand in hand, we walked into her trunk.

My head pounded like someone was smacking me with a hammer. Was the headache a sign we were sharing Jo's body, despite everything? Steeling myself, I opened my—our?—eyes to confront the truth.

Jo lay beside me. I was me!

Jo gripped my fingers tighter and yawned. We'd been holding hands when I fell asleep. Was that how I'd gotten back to myself?

"S'it breakfast yet?" she grumbled. "I'm starved."

"Jo!" cried Eddy.

"Pina!" yelled Arish.

They both tackled us in a giant group hug. Jo groaned, but I laughed and hugged them back.

"You did it!" said Eddy. "Your plan worked!"

"I wouldn't want you to think I'm not impressed," said Good Guy George.

"Charlie is heavier than he looks," complained Bethany. "I broke a nail getting him over here!"

Jo sat up. "What happened? What plan?"

The grass was wet, covered by a thick brown powder. It smelled like Christmas at my grandparents'. Nearby lay Ms. Angela and her brother, Charlie—the others brought him while I was under because, I reasoned, even if he couldn't return to it, having his body might give us a chance to eject him from Jo's.

In the dawn light, Charlie's pale cheeks turned him ghostly, making him look less like a kid and more like a corpse. At least the mushrooms on his body had burst. Yellow-green goop oozed out of the remains. Yuck.

"Cinnamon has antifungal properties." I stood up and brushed off my damp shorts. Jo got up to brush herself down too. "Mushrooms are like fungus fruits, so where there's mushrooms, there's fungi. I figured the Glade

THE GLADE

wouldn't like having cinnamon around, and that it might be enough to break Charlie's hold on you."

"So we dissolved cinnamon in water, like Pina said!" Arish leapt to his feet. "It was like making potions! I wanted to mix up so many things, but Bethany said I couldn't."

Bethany crossed her arms. "That's right!"

"We weren't sure it was enough," added Eddy. "George went back and grabbed more water while the rest of us sprinkled the whole case of cinnamon on the ground, and then he splashed everything. I guess it worked!"

George's eyes were glued on Ms. Angela, his chest moving fast. "Uff-da. This will be . . . interesting to explain."

"No, it won't." Bethany tossed her ponytail. "You know what Daddy says: aliens. They brought back the little boy who went missing all those years ago, and he wanted to take Angela back with him on the spaceship."

Eddy rolled his eyes, but Arish eagerly threw out other suggestions.

Jo and I looked at each other. Things had changed between us. I'd saved her and proven I could save myself. And she knew that no matter where we went, she'd always have a home with me.

Jo reached for my hand, and I took it. We turned to the sleeping siblings. Charlie's body was sprawled as if he was reaching for Ms. Angela. They might both be confined to his body, or maybe they were caught in an in-between place. If they'd been touching like Jo and I had been, that might have brought one or both of them back—but they hadn't been. Wherever Angela and Charlie were now, we couldn't help them.

"Well," I said. "At least they're together."

EPILOGUE

- One Year Later -

"Girls," said Mom from the sliding door. "Wait, sorry, still getting used to it. Kids, did you want to come to the nursery with me?"

"No thanks, Mom," I said. "These weeds won't pluck themselves! I wrote down what I needed on the list. Make sure to get the usual brands, okay? If they're out, we can go another time."

Jo grinned, the new cap I'd gotten them backward on their head. "Thanks, Mrs. A!"

Mom popped her head out, her purse already slung over her shoulder. "All right, then. I'll pick up lunch on the way home—any requests?"

"Too bad there's no deep dish places up here," I said. "Mom, can we go down to Chicago before Jo goes back?"

"We can get pizza here, Proserpina." She gave me a Mom Look, but I'd lost track of the numbers.

I shrugged. "Not deep dish. I thought you were gonna call me Pina more."

She sighed. "You're right, I did promise to try. Everything's so different now. Jo's not a girl, and you've both grown up."

Jo wrinkled their nose. They'd gotten the "this is hard" speech a bunch of times from lots of people. The week before they'd arrived, I made my parents practice with me every day, and they still messed up. When Jo had told their aunt and uncle, their guardians had flipped out and said nasty things. It was extra important that Mom and Baba got Jo's pronouns right when their aunt and uncle were doing what they always did.

It wasn't fair. Jo deserved to be in a better home. If the three of them moved back here, I hoped I could convince Mom to let Jo move in with us. Mom and Baba weren't perfect, but they wouldn't be mean on purpose.

Jo had asked me not to say anything to my parents, but every time they told me about another fight, I

THE GLADE

wavered. Their guardians did not make Jo feel safe—not about their gender, not about their parents, not about being Filipino. During the move Jo had found dozens of letters from their dad's family that had been hidden in their aunt's closet. Jo had been furious, but confronting their guardians would have made it worse. To be safe, they used my address to write letters to their grandparents in the Philippines. I took pictures of the replies for them (though, since Jo was visiting, I'd given them the original letters), and recently Jo started emailing their cousins.

"How about frozen custard, Mrs. A?" suggested Jo. Mom was strict with what she ate, but she couldn't resist frozen custard.

Mom gave us a tired smile. "I guess I can't say no to that. See you girls—kids in a bit."

I returned to my work as Mom headed out. Baba was out of town for a work trip, so it was the three of us for the couple of weeks that Jo was in town. Yesterday I'd finally convinced Jo that we should talk to my parents about their home life. We were waiting for Baba to get back tomorrow.

"What a year, huh?" Jo lay on the grass. They didn't like being outside anymore, not like they used to, but they'd been okay keeping me company in the garden. "Can't believe this time last year, we were fighting giant spiders. It feels like a dream."

After Jo and their family moved, we stopped talking about what had happened at Camp Clear Skies. With Ms. Angela and her brother in comas, George and the other counselors called guardians for an early pickup. We'd helped drag both Angela and Charlie to Angela's cabin and put them to bed, and George said he'd use his Eagle Scout training to handle the rest. Who knew what had happened to them since, and to the Glade.

I hoped no kid would have to go through what we did. My nightmares had become more frequent. Images of the human spider. Of Charlie's mushroom body. Of being confined in the stem-trunk and my own skin. Based on both of us waking up in the middle of the night during this visit, I knew Jo was having nightmares too. We didn't talk about it. Instead, we held hands until we fell back asleep.

"I know, right?" I dug my fingers into the dirt to get a weed by the roots. "You said Eddy is visiting when you get back, right?"

"Yeah! His dad has a business trip in Detroit, so he's

coming with." They shielded their face from the hot summer sun. "The last time I talked to him, he said Arish's family was thinking about moving from Minneapolis. Maybe they'll be closer."

"That'd be nice." I grinned. "If his sisters don't kill him first." Now that I had a phone, Arish sent me regular texts about his latest hijinks. One day our friend might calm down his antics, but not anytime soon.

For the next few minutes, Jo lay in the grass, and I weeded the garden, moving on to new patches.

"You're really okay without me, aren't you?" said Jo, their voice quiet. "Keri pa ba, huh?" Jo's cousin André wrote them lots of emails and taught them that new word for "kaya."

We didn't use the code words that much anymore, so I stopped what I was doing and came over to sit next to them. "That doesn't mean I don't need you. I miss you always. I hope Uncle Brock gets transferred back here." Or that my parents could take Jo in. "I just don't need you to rescue me anymore, you know?"

Jo turned their cheek to look up at me, a sad smile on their face. "Yeah, I hear you. I'm proud of you, P. You kicked serious butt."

I smiled. "We both did. Hey, do you mind digging out the lemonade? I'm ready for air-conditioning."

Jo got up from the ground, brushing off their butt. They shifted their weight. "I meant what I said about it being like a dream," they said. "The Glade. Sometimes it's like I'm back there, or like I've crossed the river again. Or like someone is crawling under my skin and controlling my body like a puppet."

I stood up and took Jo's hand. "I'll come save you every time. Spiders and creepy kids with broken nursery rhymes can't keep me away."

Jo smiled for real and flicked my nose before heading inside. Things were different—*we* were different. But different didn't have to mean bad, even when it was scary. I liked the way Mom and I could talk about how both of us had anxiety, and how we could manage it without hurting each other. I liked the way I could stand up for myself. Schoolyard bullies were small fries compared to the Glade.

Deep inside me I knew neither Jo nor I were 100 percent okay. We might not be for a long, long time—if ever. The details of what had happened last year were getting hazier, but the feelings remained. The sour taste of my fear. The slither of fog on my skin.

But if I let what happened rule my life, I'd never be able to do anything difficult again. There'd be times—probably lots of times—when I'd forget. When I'd be trapped inside my head, reliving how it had felt pushing through the Glade's deceptions. (I couldn't be in small, dark places anymore.) But even if that kept happening until I got old, I didn't want to not live my life. I didn't want Jo to stay stuck either.

The garden looked good. Mom had let me take over a bigger patch this year. I surveyed the dirt around me. I'd gotten most of the weeds, except . . .

Behind my *Rhododendron* bush sprouted a cluster of soft brown mushrooms, the ones hard to identify. They looked normal and weren't stinky, and they were a sign of healthy soil. But there was no way I'd leave the cluster to grow and spread.

I crushed it underfoot.

ACKNOWLEDGMENTS

I'd like to open by acknowledging that I work on and reside in traditional territories belonging to The People who inhabited the Great Basin area: the Numa/Numu (Northern Paiute), the Washeshu (Washoe), the Newe (Shoshone), and the Nuwuvi (Southern Paiute) peoples. The Numa, Washeshu, and Newe peoples organizationally operate in Washoe County as the Reno-Sparks Indian Colony.

Writing the acknowledgments is one of my favorite parts of a project. My name might be on the cover, but so many people behind the scenes have worked tirelessly on this book's behalf. I'm so happy to spend a

ACKNOWLEDGMENTS

moment (or many pages) thanking those people.

First, to my agent, Erica Bauman: I could not imagine having a better creative or business partner. On this rocky path of ours, I cling to your constant affirmations and thoughtful responses to my panicked emails.

Without John Cusick and Mary Cole, the minds behind Upswell Media, Pina and co. would never have become such an important part of my life. Thank you for trusting me to tell this story, and to tell it my way.

When I first met my editor, Alyson Heller, I felt so lucky that I'd found someone who so strongly believed in my vision for *The Glade*. I was even luckier that Aly is a deft, thoughtful editor who helped me bring that vision to life. I am so proud of this book that we created together. Thank you for championing it.

Pina and Jo's code words were Aly's idea, but it was because of André Adricula that we found the right ones for Jo. (I slipped you a small gift in the epilogue!) "Kaya" can refer to one's capacity to endure and carry on, and "keri" is the loose bekimon equivalent. I could not think of two more perfect words to capture Jo's journey. Thank you also to Kaitlyn San Miguel for explaining how Tagalog speakers would actually use

ACKNOWLEDGMENTS

the phrase. Jo doesn't yet have the linguistic knowledge to discuss the nuances of translation (and neither do I), so I did my best to honor the original intention of using "kaya" while updating Pina's understanding of it and Jo's response to "khoobee?" (Based on what I learned, "khoobam" is probably not the best response to "kaya mo ba?"—alas!) Any mistakes are my own.

I was deeply moved and inspired by Lora Senf's Blight Harbor series; I couldn't resist *The Clackity* making a cameo in chapter one. Ms. Angela's final spider creation was inspired by Pretty Penny's (multiple) good and fair deals.

I might not have been in the room where it happened, but I know the team at Aladdin and Simon & Schuster Children's shepherded this book through the publishing process: Valerie Garfield, Kristin Gilson, Anna Jarzab, Karin Paprocki, Sara Berko, Maryam Ahmad, and Art Morgan. The delightfully spooky cover was drawn by Marcela Bolívar; thank you for centering Pina's Persian features. The book's interior was designed by Mike Rosamilia. A big shout-out to my copyeditor, Kimberly Capriola, who wrangled my commas and awkward phrasings; and to my proofreader, Jasmine Ye; and

ACKNOWLEDGMENTS

cold reader, Kaitlyn San Miguel—sorry for the spidery nightmares!

I am grateful to every bookseller, book blogger, book-various-social-media-er, book club, book box, reader, and writer who championed my adult debut. It's because of you that I'm able to continue to create and move into new realms (like this one). I'd also like to thank everyone who participated in *The Glade*'s cover reveal: Karis Rogerson, Roxanne, kitaabeinaursukoon, Wildflower Reads, Alexx, Shinyfluff, Mia P. Manansala, June T Adria, Andy, Emma/bookishemmaa, Xan, Kat, BlueSkyReview, @books_and_ketab, Peter Adrian Behravesh, @lyriahnam, Mirto, @allmyfriendsareinbooks, Alenka, Griffin Peralta, Phoebe, Jenni C, stardustandrockets, Mona, shelvesofsanity, @QueerAFictionado, K.S. Walker, Steph Suber, Stephanie, Renee Christopher, Caoilfhionn, and Blue. Some of you are friends of mine, (hit me up for coffee [my treat] whenever I next see you), but it astonished me that many more were fans of my work who wanted to help—that is deeply humbling. Kaiqi, your preorder-incentive art is marvelous! Every update made me dance for joy.

I'm also lucky to have many author and publishing

ACKNOWLEDGMENTS

friends who have similarly inspired me to keep going; I could never list you all, but I particularly want to thank Charlie Jane Anders, Annalee Newitz, Arley Sorg, and Adib Khorram for welcoming me with open arms every time they see me (physically and online). Charlie Jane, your constant belief in me has meant the world. Adib, your doogh opinions might be wrong (more for me though), but I will still scream to everyone about your work.

Speaking of doogh: the Persian Posse group and its corresponding Discord has connected me to my diasporic community in a way I never thought possible. Shouka, thank you for cultivating a space where we can all revel in our culture and the stories we create from within it, and for your unending excitement and support for Iranian authors.

I never expected that meeting Nicole Shawan Junior as a Lambda Fellow back in 2019 would have such a profound effect on my life and career. To Nicole, the Roots. Wounds. Words. team at large, and both of my speculative fiction cohorts: being RWW faculty kept me afloat through some rough periods, including when I was working on this story.

ACKNOWLEDGMENTS

My teammates (and future business partners!) at Sword & Kettle Press, Kay Marlow Allen and Jude Robinson, have been such rock stars. I love the work we do. I'm so excited for where we'll go next.

While working on *The Glade*, I became involved in several organizations that are now key to my work. Authors Against Book Bans, I'm proud to be your Nevada chapter co-lead. Freedom to Read Nevada and Washoe County librarians, I will continue to fight for and alongside you.

I feel very lucky that my FtR-NV co-organizers have also become good friends who have helped me weather various storms: Ilya Arbatman, Rosie Zuckerman, Georgia Russell, Tara de Queiroz, Gail Townsend, Jessica Munger, and Bri Schmidt. The failure of WC-1 was more tolerable because we were in it together. Additionally, Ilya and Rosie's bookstore, the Radical Cat, has become my second home. Thanks for hosting all our Heretics' Workshop events and letting me hang around every week to write. You're stuck with me!

Without the support of my loved ones, *The Glade* would never have happened. In addition to those already listed, I want to thank Renee Christopher (again, but

ACKNOWLEDGMENTS

separately from the cover reveal!), Brontë Wieland, and Vida Gomez for putting up with my nonsense. Bri, you get extra love for affirming my ADHD and OCD (hooray?) and helping me navigate the daily realities of neurodivergence and chronic illness, and for your unending enthusiasm for me and my work, and for all your help with *The Glade* marketing and promo stuffs, and for being my friend. Morgan Dunwoodie, thank you for constantly affirming me. Kathleen Kuo, I'm so glad our paths have come back together. Jennie Kaplan and Katherine Brandt, thank you both for loving me from afar. I know Michelle Aucoin Wait, Bryant Wait, and Linzy Garcia think of me as constantly and fondly as I do y'all. Misha and Elise Grifka Wander, you are my siblings in everything but blood. Sorry, everyone, that I'm such a terrible texter. Apparently, it's the ADHD.

December Cuccaro, you are my brain cell. Without you, I'd be completely dysfunctional, and the Heretics straight-up wouldn't exist. I will never cease to be amazed by your animal facts, your writing, and your care.

Terry J. Benton-Walker, being around you energizes me. Your books are a blessing to everyone who reads them. (I decided Pina's latest library find was *Alex Wise*

ACKNOWLEDGMENTS

and adjusted the first mention accordingly.) You will always have me in your corner, no matter what happens.

Maman, Baba, and Seena: Every day I'm apart from you is another day I grieve. Home is not home without you, and I miss you constantly. I love you. Everything I do, I do with you, my family, in mind, hoping to make you proud.

Liliana Bilbao, it's because of you that the love of my life is such a tender, thoughtful, caring human. Gabe, there is nothing I can write here that I have not said a thousand times over. I'm so lucky that you're my person, and that I'm yours. I couldn't do this without you.

And finally, to you, dear reader: Pina's misadventures would be little more than words on a page without you. Pina, Jo, Eddy, and Arish believe in you. So do I.

ABOUT THE AUTHOR

Naseem Jamnia (they/them) is a Markowitz Award–winning author who writes speculative fiction for adults, teens, and kids. Their adult work has been nominated for the Crawford, Locus, and World Fantasy awards, and they contributed to the YA horror anthology *The White Guy Dies First: 13 Scary Stories of Fear and Power*. Like Pina, Naseem is an Iranian American, is a trained scientist, and has always wanted to go to a sleepaway camp; unlike Pina, Naseem no longer practices neuroscience, both of Naseem's parents are Iranian immigrants, and Naseem was born and raised in Chicago. Naseem currently lives outside Reno, Nevada, with their geologist husband and four furred creatures. *The Glade* is their middle-grade debut. Find out more and join their newsletter at NaseemWrites.com or on Instagram @jamsternazzy.